There was nothing to do but surrender. To the molten fire that rolled through her. To the heaviness in her breasts, pressed hard against his chest. And to that restless, edgy, weighted thing that sank low into her belly and then pulsed hot.

Needy. Insistent.

And Kathryn *forgot*.

She forgot who he was. That she had been his stepmother for two years even though he was some eight years older than she was. She forgot that in addition to being her harshest critic and her bitter enemy, through no fault of her own Luca was now going to be her boss.

She forgot everything but the taste of him. That harsh, sweet magic he made…the way he commanded her and compelled her—as if he knew the things her body wanted and could do when she had no idea. When she was simply lost—adrift in the fire.

USA TODAY bestseller and RITA® Award-nominated author **Caitlin Crews** loves writing romance. She teaches her favourite romance novels in creative writing classes at places like UCLA Extension's prestigious Writers' Programme, where she finally gets to utilise the MA and PhD in English Literature she received from the University of York in England. She currently lives in California, with her very own hero and too many pets. Visit her at caitlincrews.com.

Visit the Author Profile page
at millsandboon.co.uk for more titles.

CASTELLI'S
VIRGIN WIDOW

BY
CAITLIN CREWS

First published in Great Britain 2016
By Mills & Boon, an imprint of HarperCollins*Publishers*
1 London Bridge Street, London, SE1 9GF

© 2016 Caitlin Crews

ISBN: 978-0-263-26354-1

Printed and bound in Great Britain
by CPI Antony Rowe, Chippenham, Wiltshire

CASTELLI'S
VIRGIN WIDOW

To my wonderful editor Flo Nicoll
for our fantastic year together!

Thank you so much for taking such great care of me—
and my books!

CHAPTER ONE

"PLEASE TELL ME this is a bad attempt at levity, Rafael.
A practical joke from the least likely clown in Italy."

Luca Castelli made no attempt to temper his harsh
tone or the scowl he could feel on his face as he glared
across the private library at his older brother. Rafael
was also his boss and the head of the family company,
a state of affairs that usually did not trouble Luca at all.

But there was nothing *usual* about today.

"I wish that it was," Rafael said from where he sat in
an armchair in front of a bright and cheerful fire that did
nothing at all to dispel Luca's sense of gloom and fury.
"Alas. When it comes to Kathryn, we have no choice."

His brother looked like a monk carved from stone
today, his features hewn from granite, which only added
to Luca's sense of betrayal and sheer *wrongness*. That
was the old Rafael, that heavy, joyless creature made
entirely of bitterness and regret. Not the Rafael of the
past few years, the one Luca greatly preferred, who
had married the love of his life he'd once thought dead
and was even now expecting his third child with her.

Luca hated that grief had thrown them all so far back
into unpleasant history. Luca hated grief, come to that.
No matter its form.

Their father, the infamous Gianni Castelli, who had built an empire of wine and wealth and brusque personality that spanned at least two continents, but was better known around the world for his colorful marital life, was dead.

Outside, January rain lashed the windows of the old Castelli manor house that sprawled with such insouciance at the top of an alpine lake in Northern Italy's Dolomite Mountains, as it had done for generations. The heavy clouds were low over the water, concealing the rest of the world from view, as if to pay tribute to the old man as he'd been interred in the Castelli mausoleum earlier this morning.

Ashes rendered ashes and dust forever dust.

Nothing would ever be the same again.

Rafael, who had been acting CEO of the family business for years now despite Gianni's blustery refusal to formally step aside, was now indisputably in charge. That meant Luca was the newly minted chief operating officer, a title that did not come close to describing his pantheon of responsibilities as co-owner but was useful all the same. Luca had initially thought these finicky bits of official business were a good thing for the Castelli brothers as well as the company, not to mention long overdue, given they'd both been acting in those roles ever since the start of their father's decline in health some years back.

Until now.

"I fail to understand why we cannot simply pay the damned woman off like all the rest of the horde of ex-wives," Luca said, aware that his tone was clipped and bordering on unduly aggressive. He felt restless and edgy in his position on the low couch opposite Rafael, but he knew if he moved, it would end badly. A fist through a wall. An upended bookshelf. A broken pane of glass. All highly charged reactions he did not care to explore, much less explain to his brother—given they smacked of a loss of control, which Luca did not allow. Ever. "Settle some of Father's fortune on her, send her on her way and be done with it."

"Father's will is very clear in regard to Kathryn," Rafael replied, and he sounded no happier about it than Luca felt. Luca told himself that was something anyway. "And she is his widow, Luca. Not his ex-wife. A crucial distinction."

Luca nearly growled but checked it at the last moment. "That's nothing but semantics."

"Sadly not." Rafael shook his head, but his gaze never left Luca's. "The choice is hers. She can either accept a lump settlement now, or a position in the company. She chose the latter."

"This is ridiculous."

It was something far worse than merely ridiculous, but Luca didn't have a word to describe that gnawing, hollow thing inside him that always yawned open at any mention of his father's sixth and final wife. *Kathryn.*

The one who was even now in the larger, more formal library downstairs, crying what appeared to be real tears over the death of a husband three times her age she could only have married for the most cynical of reasons. Luca had seen them trickle silently down her cheeks, one after the next, as they'd all stood about in the frigid air earlier, giving the impression she could not manage to contain her grief.

He didn't believe it. Not for a second.

If Luca knew anything, it was this: the kind of love

that might lead to such grieving was rare, exceedingly unlikely and had never made a great many appearances in the Castelli family. He thought Rafael's current happiness was perhaps the only evidence of it in generations.

"For all we know, Father found her hawking her wares on the streets of London," he muttered now. Then glared at his brother. "What the hell will I do with her in the office? Do we even know if she can read?"

Rafael shifted, the dark eyes that were so much like Luca's own narrow and shrewd. "You will find something to keep her busy, because the will assures her three years of employment. Ample time to introduce her to the joys of the written word, I'd think. And whether you like her or not is irrelevant."

Like was not at all the word Luca would have used to describe what happened inside him at the mention of that woman. It wasn't even close.

"I have no feelings about her whatsoever." Luca let out a laugh that sounded hollow to his own ears. "What is one more child bride—acquired solely to cater to the old man's ego—to me?"

His brother only gazed at him for a moment that seemed to stretch on for far too long. The old windows rattled. The fire crackled and spat. And Luca found he had no desire whatsoever to hear whatever his older brother might say next. He'd preferred Rafael when he'd been lost in a prison of fury and regret, he told himself, and unable to concentrate on anything outside his own pain. At least then he'd been a known quantity. This new Rafael was entirely too insightful.

"If you are determined to do this," he said before Rafael could open his mouth and say things Luca would have to fend off, "why not set her up with something in Sonoma? She can get a hands-on experience at the vineyards in California, just as we did when we were boys. It can be a delightful holiday for her, far, far away."

From me, he did not say. *Far, far away from me.*

Rafael shrugged. "She chose Rome."

Rome. Luca's city. Luca's side of their highly competitive wine business. The marketing power and global reach of the Castelli Wine brand were, he flattered himself, all his doing—and possible in large part because he'd been left to his own devices for years. He had certainly not been required to play babysitter for one of his father's legion of mistakes.

His father's very worst mistake, to his way of thinking. In a lifetime of so very many—including Luca himself, he'd long thought. He knew his father would have agreed.

"There's no room," he said now. "The team is lean, focused and entirely handpicked. There's no place for a bit of fluff on sabbatical from her true vocation as an old man's trophy."

Rafael was his boss then, he could see. Not his brother.

And entirely pitiless. "You'll have to make room."

Luca shook his head. "It may set us back months, if not years, and cause incalculable damage in the process as we try to arrange the team around such a creature and what are sure to be her many, many mistakes."

"I trust you'll ensure that none of that happens," Rafael said drily. "Or do you doubt your own abilities?"

"This sort of vulgar nepotism will likely cause a riot—"

"Luca." Rafael's voice was not loud, but it silenced

Luca all the same. "Your objections are noted. But you are not seeing the big picture."

Luca tried to contain the seething thing within that pushed out from the darkest part of him and threatened to take him over. He thrust his legs out in front of him and raked a hand through his hair as if he was languid. Indolent. Unbothered by all of this, despite his arguments.

The role he'd been playing all his life. He had no idea why it had become so difficult these past couple of years to maintain his profoundly unconcerned facade. Why it had started to feel as if it was more of a cage than a retreat.

"Enlighten me," he said, mildly enough, when he was certain he could manage to speak in his usual half bored, half amused tone.

Rafael did not look fooled. But he only picked up his glass from the antique side table and swirled the amber liquid within.

"Kathryn has captured the public's interest," he said after a moment. "I shouldn't have to remind you of that. *Saint Kate* has been on every cover of every tabloid since the news of Father's death broke. Her grief. Her selflessness. Her true love for the old man against all odds. Et cetera."

"You will excuse me if I am skeptical about the truth of her devotion." At least he sounded far more amused than he felt. "To put it mildly. The truth of her interest in his bank account I find a far more convincing tale, if less entertaining."

"The truth is malleable and has little to do with the story that ends up splashed across every gossip site and magazine in existence," Rafael said, and there was the hint of a rueful smile on his face when he looked at Luca again. "No one knows this better than me. Can we really complain if this time the coverage is not exactly in our favor?"

Luca wasn't sure he found his latest stepmother's obvious manipulation of the press to be in the same realm as the stories Rafael and his wife, Lily—who also happened to be their former stepsister, because the Castelli family tree was nothing if not tangled and bent back on itself—had told to explain the fact she'd been thought dead for five years.

But he thought better of saying anything.

After a moment, Rafael continued, "The reality is this. Even though you and I have been running things for years now, the perception from the outside is very different. Father's death gives anyone and everyone the opportunity to make grand claims about how his upstart, ungrateful sons will ruin what he built. If we are seen to shun Kathryn, to treat her badly, that can only reflect negatively on us and add fuel to that fire." He set his glass down without drinking from it. "I want no fuel, no fire. Nothing the tabloids can sink their dirty little claws into. You understand. This is necessary."

What Luca understood was that this was a directive. From the chief executive officer of Castelli Wine and the new official head of his family to one among his many underlings. The fact that Luca owned half of the company did not change the fact he answered to Rafael. And that none of this sat well with him didn't alter the fact that Rafael wasn't asking his opinion on the matter.

He was delivering an order.

Luca stood abruptly, before he said things he wasn't

sure he meant in an effort to sway his brother's opinion. Rafael stayed where he was.

"I don't like this," Luca said quietly. "It can't end well."

"It must end well," Rafael countered. "That's the whole point."

"I'll remind you that this was entirely your idea when it becomes a vast and unconquerable disaster, sinking the whole of Castelli Wine in the wake of this woman's incompetence," Luca said, and started for the door. He needed to *do* something. Run for miles and miles. Swim even farther. Lift very heavy weights or find a willing and eager woman. Anything but stay here and brood about this terrible new reality. "We can discuss it as we plummet to the bottom of the sea. In pieces."

Rafael laughed.

"Kathryn is not our Titanic, Luca," he said, and there was a note Luca did not like at all in his voice. Rafael tilted his head slightly to one side. "But perhaps you think she's yours?"

What Luca thought was that he could do without his brother's observations today—and on any day, should those observations involve Kathryn, who was without doubt the bane of his existence.

Damn that woman. And damn his father for foisting her upon his sons in the first place.

He left Rafael behind in the private library with a rude hand gesture that made his brother laugh, and headed downstairs through the grand old hallways of the ancient house that he hardly noticed the details of anymore. The portraits cluttering the walls. The statuary by this or that notable Italian artist flung about on every flat surface. It was all the same as it had been before Luca had been born, and the same as it would be when Rafael's eldest son, Arlo, was a grandfather. Castellis endured, no matter the messes they made.

He imagined that meant he would, too, despite this situation.

Somehow.

He heard Lily's voice as he passed one of the reception rooms and glanced in, seeing his pregnant sister-in-law, some six months along, having one of her "discussions" with eight-year-old Arlo and two-year-old Renzo about appropriate behavior. Luca hid a grin as he passed, thinking the lecture sounded very similar to ones he'd received in the very same place when he'd been a child. Not from his mother, who had abdicated that position as quickly as possible following Luca's birth, or from his father, who had been far too important to trouble himself with domestic arrangements or child rearing. He'd been raised by a parade of well-meaning staff and a series of stepmothers with infinitely more complicated motives.

Perhaps that was where he'd learned his lifelong aversion to complications.

And to stepmothers, for that matter.

Luca had grown up in the midst of a very messy family who'd broadcasted their assorted private dramas for all the world to see, no matter if the relentless publicity had made it all that much worse. He'd hated it. He preferred things clean and easy. Orderly. No fusses. No melodrama. No theatrics that ended up splashed across the papers, the way everything always did in the Castelli family, and were then presented in the most hideous light imaginable. He didn't mind that he was seen as one of the world's foremost playboys—hell, he'd cul-

tivated that role so no one would ever take him seriously, an asset in business as well as in his personal
life. He didn't break hearts—he simply didn't traffic
in the kind of emotional upheavals that had marked
every other member of his family, again and again and
again. *No, thank you.*

But Kathryn was a different story, he thought as he
made his way to the grand library on the ground floor
and saw the slight figure standing all alone in the farthest corner, staring out at the rain and the fog as if she
was competing with it for the title of Most Desolate.
Kathryn was more than a mess.

Kathryn was a disaster.

He wasn't the least bit surprised that *Saint Kate*, as
she'd been dubbed around the world for her supposed
martyrdom to the cause that was old Gianni Castelli
and his considerable fortune, was all over the papers
this week. Kathryn did *convincingly innocent* and *easily wounded* so well that Luca had always thought she'd
have been much better off dedicating her life to the
stage.

Though he supposed she had, really. Playing the understanding mistress and undemanding trophy wife to
a man so much older than her twenty-five years was a
performance all its own. What Luca couldn't understand was why an obvious trollop like Kathryn made
his skin feel too tight against his frame and his hands
itch to test the smoothness of hers, even now. It didn't
make any sense, this stretched-taut, heavy *thing* in him
that nothing—not time, not space, not the odious fact
of her marriage to his own father, not even the prospect
of her polluting the refuge of his office in Rome—ever
eased or altered in any way.

He glared at her from the doorway, down the length of the great room with so many books lining the floor-to-ceiling shelves, as if he could make it disappear. Or barring that, make *her* disappear.

But he knew better.

It had always been like this.

Luca's father had made a second career out of marrying a succession of unsuitable younger women who'd let him act the savior. He'd thrived on it. Gianni had never had much time for his sons or the first wife he'd shunted out of sight into a mental institution and mourned very briefly after her death, if at all. But for his parade of mistresses and wives with their endless needs and worries and crises and melodramas? He had been always and ever available to play the benevolent God, solver of all calamities, able to sort out all manner of troubles with a wave of his debit card.

When Gianni had arrived back in Italy a scant month after his fifth wife had divorced him with his sixth wife in tow, Luca hadn't been particularly surprised.

"There is a new bride," Rafael had told him darkly when Luca had arrived in the Dolomites as summoned that winter morning two years ago. "Already."

Luca had rolled his eyes. What else was there to do?

"Is this one of legal age?"

Rafael had snorted. "Barely."

"She's twenty-three," the very pregnant Lily had said reprovingly, her hands on the protruding belly that would shortly become Renzo. She'd glared at both of them. "That's hardly a child. And she seems perfectly nice."

"Of course she seems nice," Rafael had retorted, and had only grinned at the look Lily had thrown at him, the connection between them as bright and shining as ever, as if Castellis could actually make something good from one of their grand messes after all. "That is her job, is it not?"

Luca had prepared himself for a stepmother much like the last occupant of the role, the sharp blonde creature whom Gianni had inexplicably adored despite the fact she'd spent more time on her mobile or propositioning his sons than she had with him. Corinna had been nineteen when she'd married Gianni and already a former swimsuit model. Luca hadn't imagined his father had chosen her for her winning personality or depth of character.

But instead of another version of fake-breasted and otherwise entirely plastic Corinna, when he'd strode into the library where his father waited with Arlo, he'd found Kathryn.

Kathryn, who should not have been there.

That had been his first thought, like a searing blaze through his mind. He'd stopped, thunderstruck, halfway across the library floor and scowled at the woman who'd stood there smiling politely at him in that reserved British way of hers. Until his inability to do anything but glower at her had made that curve of her lips falter, then straighten into a flat line.

She doesn't belong here, he'd thought again, harsher and more certain. Not standing next to his old, crotchety father tucked up in his armchair before the fire, all wrinkles and white hair and fingers made of knots, thanks to years of arthritis. Not wringing her hands together in front of her like some kind of awkward schoolgirl instead of resorting to the sultry, come-hither glances Luca's stepmothers normally threw his way.

Not his *stepmother.*

That thought had been the loudest.

Not her.

Her hair was an inky dark brown that looked nearly black, yet showed hints of gold when the firelight played over it. It poured down past her shoulders, straight and thick, and was cut into a long fringe over smoky-gray eyes that edged toward green. She wore a simple pair of black trousers and a cleanly cut caramel-colored sweater open over a soft knit top that made no attempt whatsoever to showcase her cleavage. She looked elegantly efficient, not plastic or cheap in any way. She was small and fine boned, all big gray eyes and that dark hair and then, of course, there was her mouth.

Her mouth.

It was the mouth of a sulky courtesan, full and suggestive, and for a long, shocking moment, Luca had the strangest notion that she had no idea of its carnal wallop. That she was an innocent—but that had been absurd, of course. Wishful thinking, perhaps. No *innocent* married a very rich man old enough to be her own grandfather.

"Luca," Gianni had barked, in English for his new wife's benefit. "What is the matter with you? Show some manners. Kathryn is my wife and your new stepmother."

It had filled Luca with a kind of terrible smoke. A black, choking fury he could not have named if his life had depended upon it.

He hadn't been aware that he was moving, only that he'd been across the room and then was right there in front of her, looming over her, dwarfing her with his superior height and size—

Not that she'd backed down. Not Kathryn.

He'd seen far too much in those expressive eyes of hers, wide with some kind of distress. And awareness— he'd seen the flare of it, followed almost instantly by confusion. But instead of simpering or shifting her body to better advantage or sizing him up in any way, she'd squared her slender shoulders and stuck out her hand.

"Pleased to meet you," she'd said, her English-accented voice brisk. Matter-of-fact. The sound of it had fallen through him like a hail of ice and had done nothing to soothe that fire in him at all.

Luca had taken her hand, though he'd known it was a terrible mistake.

And he'd been right. It had been.

He'd felt the drag of her skin against his, palm to palm, like a long, slow lick down the length of his sex. He should have jerked his hand away. Instead, he'd held her tighter, feeling her delicacy, her heat and, more telling, that wild tumult of her pulse in her wrist. Her lips had parted as if she'd felt it, too.

He'd had to remind himself—harshly—that they were not only not alone, she was also not free.

She was something a whole lot worse than *not free*, in fact.

"It is my pleasure, *Stepmother*," he'd said, his voice low and dark, that terrible fire in him shooting like electricity all through his limbs and then into her. He'd seen her stiffen—whether in shock at his belligerence or with that same stunned awareness that stampeded in him, he'd never know. "Welcome to the family."

And it had been downhill from there.

All leading him here. To the same library, two years later, where Kathryn stood like a lonely wraith in a simple black dress that somehow made her look fragile and too pretty at once, her dark hair clipped back and no hint of color on her face below that same inky fringe that kissed the tops of her eyelashes.

She was gazing off into the distance through the windows that opened up over the lake, and she looked genuinely sad. As if she truly mourned Gianni, the man she'd used shamelessly for her own ends—ends that, apparently, included forcing herself into Luca's office against his will.

And it enraged him.

He told himself that was the thing that washed over him then, digging in its claws. *Rage.* Not that far darker, far more dangerous thing that lurked in him, as much that terrible hunger he'd prefer to deny as it was the familiar companion of his own self-loathing.

"Come, now, Kathryn," Luca said into the heavy quiet of the book-lined room, making his voice a dark and lazy thing just this side of insulting, and taking note of how she instantly stiffened against it. Against him. "The old man is dead and the reporters have gone home. Who is this maudlin performance for?"

CHAPTER TWO

LUCA CASTELLI'S TRADEMARK GROWL, his English laced with an undercurrent of both his native Italian and that particular harsh ruthlessness that Kathryn had only ever heard directed at her, jolted through her like an electric shock.

She jerked where she stood near the library window, actually jumping in a way he'd be unlikely to miss, even from all the way on the other side of the long, luxurious, stunningly appointed room.

Well done, she thought, despairing of herself anew. *Now he knows exactly how much he gets to you.*

She didn't expect that anything she did would make this man *like* her. Luca had made it clear that could never happen. Over and over and over again, these past two years. But she wanted him—*needed* him—not to actively hate her as she started this new phase of her life.

Kathryn figured that was better than nothing. As good a start as she could hope for, really. And her mother certainly hadn't raised her to be a coward, despite how disappointing she knew she'd always been. Rose Merchant had never let hardship get between her and what needed to be done, as she'd reminded Kathryn at every opportunity. Forging ahead into the corporate world the way Rose hadn't been able to do with a child to raise all on her own was, truly, the least Kathryn could do to honor all of her sacrifices.

And to assuage the guilt she felt about her marriage to Gianni—the one time "honoring her mother's sacrifices" had allowed her to do something purely for herself, too. But she couldn't let herself think about that too closely. It made her feel much too ungrateful.

Kathryn straightened from her place at the window, aware that her movements were jerky and awkward, the way she always seemed to be around this man, who noticed every last embarrassing detail about her and never hesitated to use each and every one of them against her. She nervously smoothed down the front of her dress. Nervously and also carefully, as if the dress was a talisman.

She'd agonized over what to wear today because she'd wanted to look as unlike the gold-digging whore she knew the family—*Luca*—thought she was as possible. And still, she was terribly afraid she'd ended up looking rather more like a poor man's version of an Audrey Hepburn wannabe instead. The papers would trumpet that possibility, call it *an homage to Audrey* or something equally embarrassing, and Luca would assume it was all part of a deliberate campaign toward some grim end he believed she'd been angling toward since the start, rather than simply riding out the attention as best she could. The cycle of his bitter condemnation would continue, turning and turning without end...

But she was delaying the inevitable. She'd always wanted a chance to prove herself, to work on the creative side of a corporation and try her hand at something fun and interesting like marketing or branding instead of the deadly dull figures at which she was utterly hopeless. She'd spent her whole marriage excited at the prospect of working in the family company with Luca and his creative genius.

Even if, other than that corporate flair of his, he was pretty much just awful. She assured herself powerful men often were. That Luca was run-of-the-mill in that sense.

Kathryn took a deep breath, resolutely squared her shoulders and turned to face her own personal demon at last.

"Hello, Luca," she said across the acres of space that separated them in this vast room, and she was proud of herself. She sounded so calm, so cool, when she was anything but.

For any number of reasons, but mostly because looking at Luca Castelli was like staring directly into the sun. It had been from the start.

And as usual, she was instantly dizzy.

Luca moved like a terrible shadow across the library floor, and tragically, he was as beautiful as ever. Tall and solid and impressively athletic, his rangy form was sculpted to lean, male perfection and was routinely celebrated in slick, photo-heavy tabloid exultations across at least five continents. His thick black hair always looked messy, as if he lived such a reckless, devil-may-care life that it required he run his hands through it all the time and rake it back from his darkly handsome face as punctuation to every sentence—despite the fact he was now the chief operating officer of the family company.

Even here, on the day of his father's funeral, where he wore a dark suit that trumpeted his rampant masculinity and excellent taste in equal measure, he gave off that same indolent air. That lazy, playful, perpetually relaxed state that only a man cresting high on the wealth of generations of equally affluent and pedigreed ancestors could achieve. As if no matter what he was actually doing, some part of him was always lounging about on a yacht somewhere with a cold drink in his hand and women presenting themselves for his pleasure. He had the look of a man who lived forever on the verge of laughter, deep and whole bodied, from his gorgeous mouth to his flashing dark eyes.

Kathryn had seen a hundred pictures of him exactly like that, lighting up the whole of the Amalfi Coast and half of Europe with that irrepressible *gleam* of his—

Except, of course, when he looked at her.

The scowl he wore now did nothing to make him any less beautiful. Nothing could. But it made Kathryn shake deep, deep inside, as if she'd lost control of her own bones. She wanted to bolt. She might have, if that wouldn't have made this whole situation that much worse.

Besides, if she'd learned anything these past two years, it was that there was no outrunning Luca Castelli. There was no outmaneuvering him. There was only surviving him.

"Hello, *Stepmother*," he said, that awful dark thing in his voice wrapping around her and sinking hot and blackened tendrils of something like shame into every part of her body, so deep it hurt to breathe. He seemed unaffected as ever, sauntering toward her with his usual deceptively lazy deadliness and those dark eyes so burning hot she could feel them punching into her from afar. "Or should we concoct a different title for you? *The Widow Castelli* has a certain gothic ring to it. I think. I'll have it engraved on your business cards."

"You know," Kathryn said, because she was still entirely too light-headed and not managing her tongue the way she should, "if you decided not to be horrible to me for five minutes the world wouldn't *actually* screech to a halt. We'd all survive. I promise."

His face was like stone, his full lips thin with displeasure, and he was closing the distance between them much too fast for Kathryn's peace of mind.

"I have no idea why you feel you need to bring this particular performance of yours into an office setting," he said as he drew closer. "Much less mine. I'm certain there are any number of hotel bars across Europe that cater to your brand of desperation and craven greed. You should have no trouble finding your next mark within the week."

That he could still hate her so much should not have surprised her, Kathryn knew, because Luca had been remarkably consistent in that since the day she'd arrived in Italy with Gianni two years ago. And yet, like that cold winter morning when he'd charged at her across this very same floor, dark and furious and terrifying in a way she hadn't entirely understood, it did.

Though *surprise* wasn't really the right word to describe the thing that rolled inside her, flattening everything it touched.

"I suppose the world really would end if you accepted the possibility that I might not be who you think I am," she said now, straightening her spine against the familiar rush of pointless grief that was her absurd response to the fact this angry, hateful man had never liked her. Kathryn channeled that odd, scraped-raw feeling into temper instead. "You'd have to reexamine your prejudices, and who knows what might happen then? Of course a man like you would find that scary. You have so many of them."

The truth was that she hardly knew Luca, despite two years of having forced, unpleasant interactions with him. What she did know was that he'd taken an instant and intense and noticeable dislike to her. On sight. Why she'd subsequently spent even three seconds—much less the whole of her marriage to his father—trying to convince him that he was wrong about her was a mystery to her. It no doubt spoke to deep psychological problems on her part, but then again, what about her relationship with this family didn't?

But she did know that poking at him was unwise.

Kathryn had a moment to regret the fact she'd done it anyway as Luca bore down on her, striding across the expanse of polished old floors and priceless rugs tossed here and there below rows of first editions in more languages than she'd known existed, all as smug and wealthy and resolutely untouchable as he was.

"This is as good a time as any to discuss the expectations I have for all Castelli Wine employees who work in my office in Rome." Luca's voice was dark. Cold. And as he moved toward her he regarded her with that sharpness in his eyes that made her feel...fluttery, low in her belly. "First, obedience. I will tell you when I am interested in hearing from you. If you are in doubt, you can assume I prefer you remain silent. *You* can assume that will always be the case. Second, confidentiality. If you cannot be trusted, if you are forever running off to the tabloids to give whining interviews about the many ways you have been wronged and victimized, *Saint Kate—*"

Kathryn flinched. "Please don't call me that. You know that's something the tabloids have made up."

Her mum had sniffed at the name and the image more than once, then reminded Kathryn that *she* had given Kathryn everything and received little in return, yet had never been called a saint by anyone. She'd even suggested that perhaps it had been Kathryn who'd come up with that name and that obnoxious storyline in the first place. It hadn't been.

That wasn't to say she hadn't played to it now and again. She'd always been fascinated with a good brand and widespread global marketing.

The fact that no one believed she hadn't made it all up herself, however, she found maddening. "*Saint Kate* has nothing to do with me."

"Believe me," Luca said in that quiet, horrible way of his, "I am under no delusions about you or your purity."

An actual slap would have hurt less. Kathryn blinked, managed not to otherwise react and forced herself to stay right where she was instead of reeling at that. Because his opinion of her aside, this was her chance to do something she really, truly believed she'd be good at instead of what other people thought she *ought* to be good at. She knew he hated her. She might not know why, but it didn't matter in the end. Kathryn had never wanted status or jewels or whatever the stepmothers before her had wanted from Gianni. She'd wanted this. A chance to prove herself at a job she knew she could do, in a company that had international reach and a bold, bright future, and to finally show her mother that she, too, could succeed in business. *Her* way, not Rose's way. This was what Gianni had promised her when he'd persuaded her to leave her MBA course in

London and marry him—the opportunity to work in the family business when the marriage was over.

This was what she wanted. She knew that if she did what every last nerve in her body was shrieking at her to do and broke for the door, she'd never come back, and Luca, certainly, would never give her another chance, no matter what it said in Gianni's will.

Her mother would never, ever forgive her. And the lonely little girl inside Kathryn, who had never wanted anything but Rose's love no matter how out of reach that had always been, simply couldn't let that happen.

"Luca," she said now, "before you really warm up to your insults, which are always *so* creative and comprehensive, I want to make sure you understand that I have every intention—"

"May the angels save me from the intentions of unscrupulous women." He was almost upon her, and one of the most unfair parts of this was that she couldn't seem to keep herself from feeling something like mesmerized by the way he moved. That impossible, offhanded grace of his he didn't deserve, and she shouldn't *notice* the way she did. It made her limbs feel precarious. Uncertain. "Third, my father's will says only that I must accommodate your desire to play at an office job, not what that job entails. If you complain, about anything at all, it will get worse. Do you understand?"

She felt a dark, hard pulse inside her then. It felt like running. Like fright. It gripped her, hard. In her temples. In the hollows behind her knees. In her throat.

In her sex.

Kathryn didn't have any idea what was happening to her. She struck out at him instead.

"Oh, what fun." She stared back at him when his

scowl edged over into something purely ferocious, and she made no attempt to rein in her sarcastic tone. Gianni was dead. The gloves were off. "Are you planning to make me scrub the floors? Let me guess, on my hands and knees with a toothbrush? That will teach me... something, I'm sure."

"I doubt that very much," he gritted out. He stopped a few feet away from her. *Too close*. Luca stood there then, in all his male fury while that dark thing that had always flared between them wound tighter and tighter around them and stole all the air from the graceful room. "But if I ask you to do it, whatever it is, I expect it to be done. No excuses."

Kathryn forced herself to speak. "And what if it turns out you're wrong about me and I'm not quite as useless as you imagine? I'm guessing abject apologies aren't exactly your strong suit."

His hard mouth—that she shouldn't find so *fascinating*, because what was wrong with her? She might as well find a shark cuddly—shifted into a merciless curve that was entirely too harsh to be a smile. "Have I ever told you how much I hate women like you?"

That word. *Hate*. It was a very strong word, and Kathryn had never understood how everything between them could feel so *intense*. She wasn't any clearer about that now. Nor why it scraped at that raw place inside her, as if it mattered deeply to her. As if he did.

When of course, he couldn't. He didn't. Luca was a means to an end, nothing more.

"It was rather more implied than stated outright," she replied, fighting to keep her voice even. "Nonetheless, you can take pride in the fact you managed to make your feelings perfectly clear from the start."

"My father married ever-younger women the way some men change their shoes," Luca said darkly, as if this was news to either one of them. "You are nothing but the last in his endless, pointless game of musical beds. You are not the most beautiful. You are not even the youngest. You are merely the one who survived him. You must know you meant nothing to him."

Kathryn shook her head at him. "I know exactly what I meant to your father."

"I would not brag, were I you, about your calculating and conniving ways," he threw back at her. "Especially not in my office, where you will find that the hardworking people who are rewarded on their merits rather than their various seduction techniques are unlikely to celebrate that approach."

Luca shook his head, judgment written in every line of his body in that elegant suit that a man as horrible as he was shouldn't have been able to wear so well. *Seduction techniques*, he'd said, the way someone might say *the Ebola virus*. It offended her, Kathryn thought.

He offended her.

Maybe that was why she lost her mind a little bit. He'd finally pushed her too far.

"I spent most of my marriage trying to figure out why you hated me so much," she bit out, heedless of his overwhelming proximity. Not caring the way she should about that glittering thing in his dark eyes. "That a grown man, seemingly of sound mind and obviously capable of performing great corporate feats when it suited him, could loathe another person on sight and for no reason. This made no sense to me."

She was aware of the grand house arrayed behind him, its ancient Italian splendor pressing in on her from all sides. Of the crystal clear lake that stretched off into the mist and the mountains that rose sharp and imposing above it. Of Gianni, sweet old Gianni, who she would never make laugh again and would never call her *cara* again in his gravelly old voice. Even this rarefied, beautiful world felt diminished by the loss of him, and here Luca was, as hateful as ever.

She couldn't bear it.

"I'm a decent person. I try to do the right thing. More to the point—" Kathryn raised her voice slightly when Luca made a derisive noise "—I'm not worth all the hatred and brooding you've been directing at me for years. I married your father and took care of him, the end. Neither you nor your brother had any interest in doing that. Some men in your position might *thank* me."

It was as if Luca expanded to fill the whole of the library then, he was so big, suddenly. Even bigger than he already was. So big she couldn't breathe, and he hadn't moved a muscle. He was simply dark and terrible, and that awful light in his eyes burned when he scowled at her.

"You were one more in a long line of—"

"Yes, but that's the thing, isn't it?" He looked astonished that she'd interrupted him, but Kathryn ignored that and kept going. "If you'd seen the likes of me before, why hate me at all? I should have been run-of-the-mill."

"You were. You were sixth."

"But you didn't despise the other five," Kathryn snapped, frustrated. "Lily told me all about them. You liked *her* mother. The last one tried to crawl into bed with you more than once, and you laughed each time you dumped her out in the hall. You simply told her to

stop trying because it would never happen with you—
you didn't even tell your father. You didn't hate *her*,
and you *knew* she was every single thing you accuse
me of being."

"Are you truly claiming you are not those things?
That you are, in fact, this unrecognizable paragon I've
read so much about in the papers? Come now, Kathryn.
You cannot imagine I am so naive."

"I never did anything to you, Luca," she hurled at
him, and she couldn't control her voice then.

There were nearly two years of repressed feelings
bottled up inside her. Every slight. Every snide remark.
Every cutting word he'd said to her. Every vicious, unfair glare. Every time he'd walked out of a room she
entered in obvious disgust. Every time she'd looked
up from a conversation to find that stare of his all over
her, like a touch.

It was true that on some level, it was refreshing to
meet someone who was so shockingly *direct*. But that
didn't make it hurt any less.

"I have no idea why you hated me the moment you
saw me. I have no idea what goes on in that head of
yours." She stepped forward, far too close to him and
then, no longer caring what his reaction would be, she
went suicidal and poked two fingers into his chest. Hard.
"But after today? I no longer care. Treat me the way you
treat anyone else who works for you. Stop acting as if
I'm a demon sent straight from hell to torture you."

He'd gone deathly still beneath her fingers. Like
marble.

"Remove your hand." His voice was frozen. Furious. "Now."

She ignored him.

"I don't have to prove that I'm a decent person to you. I don't care if the world knows your father forced you to hire me. I *know* I'll do a good job. My work will speak for itself." She poked him again, just as hard as before, and who cared if it was suicidal? There were worse things. Like suffering through another round of his character assassinations. "But I'm not going to listen to your abuse any longer."

"I told you to remove your hand."

Kathryn held his dark gaze. She saw the bright warning in it, and it should have scared her. It should have impressed her on some level, reminded her that whatever else he was, he was a very strong, very well built man who was as unpredictable as he was dangerous.

And that he hated her.

But instead, she stared right back at him.

"I don't care what you think of me," she told him, very distinctly.

And then she poked him a third time. Even harder than before, right there in that shallow between his pectoral muscles.

Luca moved so fast she had no time to process it.

She poked him, then she was sprawled across the hard wall of his chest with her offending hand twisted behind her back. It was more than dizzying. It was like toppling from the top of one of the mountains that ringed the lake, then hurtling end over end toward the earth.

Her heart careened against her ribs, and his darkly gorgeous face was far too close to hers and she was *touching* him, her dress not nearly enough of a barrier to keep her from noticing unhelpful things like his scent, a hint of citrus and spice. The heat that blazed from him, as if he was his own furnace. And that de-ceptively languid strength of his that made something deep inside her flip over.

Then hum.

"This, you fool," Luca bit out, his mouth so close to hers she could taste the words against her own lips. She could taste *him*, and she shuddered helplessly, com-pletely unable to conceal her reaction. "This is what I think of you."

And then he crushed his mouth to hers.

CHAPTER THREE

HE DID NOT ASK. He did not hesitate. He simply *took*.

Luca's mouth descended on hers, and Kathryn waited for that kick of terror, of unease, of sheer panic that had always accompanied any hint of male sexual interest in her direction before—

But it never came.

He kissed her with all that lazy confidence that made him who he was. He took her mouth again and again, still holding her arm behind her back and then sliding his free hand along her jaw to guide her where he wanted her.

Slick. Hot.

Deliciously, wildly, stunningly male.

He kissed her as if they'd done this a thousand times before. As if the past two years had been leading nowhere but here. To this hot, impossible place Kathryn didn't recognize and couldn't navigate.

There was nothing to do but surrender. To the molten fire that rolled through her and pooled in all the worst places. A heaviness in her breasts, pressed hard against his chest. And that restless, edgy, weighted thing that sank low into her belly and then pulsed hot.

Needy. Insistent.

And Kathryn *forgot*.

She forgot who he was. That she had been his step-mother for two years, though he was some eight years older than she was. She forgot that in addition to being her harshest critic and her bitter enemy through no fault of her own, he was now going to be her boss.

She forgot everything but the taste of him. That harsh, sweet magic he made, the way he commanded her and compelled her, as if he knew the things her body wanted and could do when she had no idea. When she was simply lost—adrift in the fire. The greedy, consuming flames that licked all over her and through her and deep inside her and made her meet every stroke of his tongue, every glorious taste—

He set her away from him. As if it hurt.

"Damn you," he muttered. Followed by something that sounded far harsher in Italian.

But it seemed to take him a very long time to let go of her.

Kathryn couldn't speak. She didn't understand the things that were storming through her then, making her blood seem like thunder in her veins and her skin seem to stretch too tight to contain all the *feelings* she didn't know how to name.

They stared at each other in the scant bit of space between them. His face was drawn tight, stark and harsh, and it still did absolutely nothing to detract from his sheer male beauty.

"You kissed me," Kathryn said, and she could have kicked herself.

But her lips felt swollen and she had the taste of him in her mouth, and she didn't know how to process that hot and slippery feeling that charged through her and then concentrated between her legs.

If possible, that dark look on his face got blacker. As if he was a storm.

"Don't you dare try that innocent game on me," he gritted out.

"I don't know what that means."

"It means I know the difference between a virgin and a whore, Kathryn," Luca said, the fury in him like a brand that pressed into her, searing her flesh, and she didn't understand how she could feel it the same way she had that desperate kiss. "I can certainly taste it."

She realized she had absolutely no idea how to respond to that.

"Luca," she said, as carefully as she could when her entire body was lost in the tumult of that endless kiss. When she had no idea how she was even capable of speech. "I think we should chalk that up as nothing more than an emotional response to a very hard day and—"

"I will not be your next target, Kathryn," Luca told her, a frozen sort of outrage in his voice and pressed deep into the fine lines of his beautiful face. "Hear me on this. *It will not happen.*"

"I don't have targets." She blinked, the room seeming to shimmer everywhere he was not, as if he was a black hole. "I'm not a weapon. What kind of life do you lead that you think these things?"

He reached over and took her upper arm in his hand, pulling her close to him again, and that fire that hadn't really banked at all blazed. Fierce and wild. Almost knocking her from her feet.

"I don't want you in my office," he growled. "I don't want you polluting the Castelli name any more than you already have. I don't want you anywhere near the things that matter to me."

Kathryn's teeth chattered, though she wasn't cold.

"That would probably be far more terrifying a threat if you weren't touching me," she managed to point out, though her voice wasn't nearly as cool as she'd have liked. "Again."

Luca laughed, though it bore no resemblance to that carefree, golden laughter that had helped make him so beloved the world over, and released her. If she didn't know better, if he'd been some other man with the usual collection of weaknesses instead of a monolith where his heart should have been, she'd have thought he hadn't meant to grab her in the first place.

"I will never lower myself to my father's discards," he told her, horribly, his gaze hard on hers in case she was tempted to pretend she hadn't heard that. "Nor will I allow you to corrupt the good people in my office with your repulsive little schemes. Your game won't work on me."

"Right," she said, and maybe it was because this was all so out of control already. Maybe that was why she couldn't seem to keep herself in check any longer around him. What was the point? She'd tried to *rise above* him for two years, and here they were anyway. "That's why you kissed me, I imagine. To demonstrate your immunity."

Luca went very still.

So still that Kathryn stopped breathing herself, as if the slightest noise might set him off. His dark eyes were fixed on her as if she was the kind of target he'd mentioned before, and she'd never felt more like one in her life. Between them, that spinning, tightening, desperate and dangerous electric band seemed to wrap tighter, pull harder. So hard it pulsed inside her, insistent and rough. So lethal she swore she could see it stamped across every tightly held, hard-packed muscle on his sculpted form.

Rain clattered against the windows behind her, and off in some other part of this massive house, little Renzo let loose one of his ear-piercing toddler screams that could as easily be joy as peril.

Luca shook his head slightly, as if he'd been released from a spell. He stepped back, his expression shifting from whatever that harsh, hard thing was to something far closer to disgust.

"You will regret this," he promised her.

She swallowed. "You'll have to be more specific. That could cover a lot of ground."

"I will make sure of it," Luca told her, as if she hadn't spoken. "If it's the very last thing I do."

His voice had the ring of a certain finality, and it clanged inside her like a gong. She stood there, stricken, her mouth still aching from his kiss and her body lost in its own strange riot, and watched as he simply turned and began to walk away from her.

She wanted nothing more than to forget all about this. To take the lump payment Rafael had offered her and disappear with it. She could have any life she wanted now. She could be anyone she wanted, far away from the long shadow of the Castellis where she'd lived for so long.

But that would mean the past two years of her life had been for nothing. That she'd simply thrown them away for cash. It would mean she was exactly the woman Luca thought she was—and that all her mother's sacrifices would have been for nothing in the end. That there was nothing to Kathryn's own life but guilt and falling short.

And Kathryn could bear a lot of things. She'd had no choice, given what a failure she'd turned out to be in her mother's eyes. She simply didn't have it in her to make it that much worse. There was that part of her that was convinced, after all this time, that if she tried hard enough she could make her mother love her. If she could just do the right thing, for once.

"I'm so glad we had this talk," she called after him, directing her not-quite-sweet tone straight toward the center of his tall, broad back. He wanted to play target practice? She could do that. "It will make Monday so much better for everyone."

He didn't turn back to face her, though he slowed. "Monday?"

If she was the good person she'd always believed herself to be, Kathryn thought then, surely she wouldn't take *quite* so much pleasure in this tiny little moment, this almost pointless victory.

"Oh, yes," she said, with deliberate calm and that triumph right there in her voice. "That's when I start."

He should never have touched her.

He should *certainly* not have tasted her.

But he had always been a fool where that woman was concerned, and in case he'd been tempted to doubt that, she haunted him all the way back to Rome.

Luca drove himself into the city from the family's private airfield, risking death in an appropriately sleek and low-slung car that made Rome's famously chaotic traffic a game of wits and daring and delicious speed. And he regretted it when he arrived at the Renaissance-era villa that housed both his business and his home, because playing games with his life at high speeds through the streets of the ancient city he loved was far preferable—and much less dangerous—than letting himself think about Kathryn.

Though he supposed both edged into that same dark place inside him, as if he was as much of a damned mess as every other Castelli in history down deep, beneath all the controls he'd spent his life putting into place to prevent exactly that.

He tossed his keys to the waiting attendant in his garage and stalked into the building, only to find himself standing stock-still in his own empty reception area, his head filled with those damned *eyes* of hers, turned a dreamy slate green after he'd kissed her, and that sulky mouth—

Luca muttered a chain of curses. He raked both his hands through his hair as he headed into the offices that sprawled across the first two levels of this lovingly maintained building in Rome's Tridente neighborhood, a mere stone's throw from the Spanish Steps and Piazza del Popolo.

His office. His one true love. The only thing he'd ever loved, in point of fact. The only thing that had ever come close to loving him back, with one success after the next.

He lived in the penthouse that rambled over the top two levels, and that was where he headed now, taking his private lift up into the rooms he'd furnished with steel and chrome, wide-open spaces and minimalist art, the better to play off the history in every bit of stone and craftsmanship in the walls and the high, frescoed ceilings and every view of gorgeous, sleepless, frenetic Rome out of his windows. He tore off his clothes in his rooftop bedroom of glass and steel before making his way out to the pool on the wraparound terrace that surrounded the master suite and offered a three-hundred-sixty-degree perspective on the Eternal City.

If Rome could stand for more than two and a half thousand years, surely Luca could survive the onslaught of Kathryn. She had no idea what she was setting herself up for. Luca was a tough boss at the best of times, demanding and fierce, and that was what the loyal employees he'd handpicked said about him to his face. What could a former trophy wife know of the corporate world? She might have some fantasy of herself as a businesswoman, but it was unlikely she'd last the week.

Of course she won't be able to handle it, he thought with something a great deal like relief—how had he failed to realize that earlier? He was called upon to indulge her whim, not alter the whole of his carefully controlled existence. The sooner she understood how ill suited she was to a life that involved more work than play, the sooner she'd drift off to find her next conquest. The problem would take care of itself.

Luca still felt edgy and entirely too messed up, despite the chill of the winter evening and the kick of the wind. Out of control. Jittery and appalled with himself. He told himself it must be grief, though he hadn't been close with his father. He might have wished, from time to very rare and sentimental time, that he'd had a better understanding of the man whose shadow had fallen over him all these years—but he never had.

Perhaps the funeral had hit him harder than he'd realized.

Because he could not understand why he'd kissed Kathryn. What the hell was the matter with him?

How could he—a man who prided himself on always, *always* keeping his life clean and trimmed down and free from anything even resembling this kind of emotional clutter—have no idea?

He dived into the pool then, cutting into the heated water and then pulling hard as he began to swim. He lost himself in the rhythm of his strokes, the weight and rush of the water against him and the growing heat in his body as he kept going, kept pushing.

Lap after lap. Then again.

He swam and he swam, he pushed himself hard, and it was no good. She was still right there, cluttering up his head, reminding him how empty he was everywhere else.

Wide gray eyes. All that dark hair and that fringe that made her seem more mysterious somehow. All of her, wedged in him like a jagged splinter he could never remove, that he'd never managed to do anything but shove in that much farther. She worried at him and worried at him and he had no idea anymore who he was when he was near her. What he might do.

Luca stopped swimming, slamming his hands down on the lip of the pool, sending water splashing everywhere.

He did not dip his quill in his company's ink, ever. He knew better than to throw grenades like that into the middle of his life. He did not touch his employees, and he certainly did not avail himself of his father's leftovers. He had been a loud, angry child often abandoned by his single living parent for months at a time in the old manor house because of the trouble he'd caused. He'd gotten over that kind of behavior while he'd still been a child. This kind of mess was precisely what he'd spent his adult life avoiding.

This was a nonissue.

Luca climbed out of the pool and wrapped himself in one of the towels his staff kept at the ready, and then made his way back inside, hardly noticing the way the sun had turned the rambling old city orange and pink as it sank toward the horizon. Not even when he stood at one of the high windows that looked out over the winding, cobbled streets that led toward Piazza di Spagna and the famous Spanish Steps, where it seemed half of Rome congregated some evenings.

He saw nothing but Kathryn, dressed in her funeral clothes like some waifish fairy tale of a widow, and it had to stop. She'd already had two black marks against her before today. Her marriage to his father in the first place. And the unpalatable fact of her tabloid presence, the endless canonization of *Saint Kate*, nauseatingly described as the plucky English lass who'd bearded any number of dragons in his twisted old-Italian family.

It repulsed him. He told himself she did, too.

That kiss today was the third black mark. He couldn't pretend he hadn't started it, hauling her to him with the kind of heedless passion he'd been so certain he'd completely excised from his life. How many times had he seen this or that foolish longing lay his father low? How often had he rolled his eyes at his brother's enduring anguish over Lily? How many times had his own pointless emotions bit him in the ass as a child? He'd promised himself a long time ago that he would stay clear of such quagmires, and the truth was, it had never been particularly difficult.

Until Kathryn. And the truth remained: he'd been the one to kiss her. He accepted that failing, even if he couldn't quite understand it.

The problem was the way she'd kissed him back.

The way she'd melted against him. The way she'd opened her mouth and met him. The way she'd poured herself into him, against him, until he'd very nearly forgotten who and where they were. That she was his stepmother, his father's widow, and that they'd been standing much too near the family mausoleum where the old man had only just been interred.

Luca was sick, there was no doubt about that—and the fact he was hard even now, at the mere memory of her taste, proved it.

But what game had she been playing?

She was good, he could admit it. She'd tasted like innocence. He still had the flavor of her on his tongue.

That was the most infuriating thing by far.

And Luca vowed, as the last bit of winter sun fell down behind Rome's enduring skyline, that he would not only make this little corporate adventure for his father's child bride of a widow as unpleasant as possible—he would also do much worse than that.

He would take Saint Kate's halo and tarnish it. And her.

Irredeemably.

By the time Kathryn made it to the ornate Castelli Wine offices in one of the most charming neighborhoods in Rome that Monday morning at exactly nine o'clock sharp, she'd prepared herself.

This was a war. A drawn-out siege. She might have lost a battle in that library far to the north in all those forbidding, foggy mountains, but that meant nothing in the scheme of things. It was a small battle. A kiss, that was all.

The war was what mattered.

The receptionist greeted her in icy Italian and pretended not to understand Kathryn's halting attempts to speak the language—then picked up the phone and spoke in flawless English, staring at Kathryn all the while. Her expression was impassive when she ended the call, but Kathryn was certain she could see triumph lurking there in the depths of the other woman's haughty gaze.

She ordered herself not to react.

"How lovely," Kathryn said, her own tone cool. "You speak English after all. Please tell Luca I'm here."

She didn't wait for the other woman's response. She went and sat in one of the rigid antique chairs that lined the waiting area and pretended to be perfectly comfortable as she waited. And waited.

And waited.

But this was a war, she reminded herself. And it had occurred to her at some point over the weekend that for all his bluster, Luca had no idea who she was or what he was dealing with. All he saw was his image of her as the gold digger who'd snared his father. That meant, Kathryn had decided, that she had the upper hand. So if he wanted to leave her stranded in purgatory all morning, cooling her heels in his waiting room as some childish gesture of pique and temper, let him. She wouldn't give him—or his receptionist, for that matter—the satisfaction of looking even the slightest bit impatient.

She kept her attention on her mobile, keeping her expression as smooth as glass as she dutifully emailed her mother to let her know she'd started work in Castelli Wine as planned, then thumbed through the news. For an hour.

When Luca finally appeared, she sensed him before she saw him. That dark, thunderous, electric thing that made every hair on her body leap to attention, filling the whole of the great cavern of a waiting room that had until that moment been bright with the Rome morning, light pouring in from the windows to dance across the marble floor. She forced herself to take her time looking up.

And there he was.

He was even more devastatingly gorgeous today, in a more casual suit than the one he'd worn at the funeral, the open white collar of his shirt offering her a far too tempting glimpse of the expanse of his olive skin and the hint of that perfect chest she knew—from the tabloid pages dedicated to him and that one Castelli family outing to Positano that had involved a boat and Luca without his shirt, God help her—had a dusting of dark hair and all those finely carved ridges in his abdomen.

She told herself she was starting to find that scowl on his face almost charming. Like a love song from an ogre.

"You're late," he said.

That was astoundingly unfair at best, but Kathryn didn't have to look to the smug receptionist to understand that there was no point arguing. Besides, Luca had warned her not to complain. She wouldn't. Kathryn stood, smoothing out her skirt as she rose.

"I apologize. It won't happen again."

"Somehow," Luca replied, sounding very nearly merry—which was alarming, "I doubt that."

Kathryn didn't bother to reply. She walked toward him, telling herself with every click of her heels against the hard floor that she remembered nothing from last week in that old library up north. Not his taste. Not that thrilling, masterful way he'd simply *taken* her mouth with his. Not the searing, impossible heat of his hand against the side of her face and that deep stroke of his clever tongue—

She hadn't dreamed those things. They hadn't kept her wide-awake and gasping at the ceiling, not sure how to handle the riot all those searing images and memories had caused inside her. *Certainly not.*

Luca's expression was unreadable as she drew close to him, and she hated that she had no idea what was going on behind his gleaming dark eyes as he ushered her deep into the heart of the Castelli Wine offices. She thought she felt him glance over her outfit, a pencil skirt and a conservative silk blouse that could offend no one, she was sure, but when she sneaked a look at him, his attention was focused straight ahead.

He stopped at the door to a large glassed-in conference room and waved a hand at the group of people sitting around the table inside. *My coworkers*, Kathryn thought—with what she realized was an utterly naive surge of pleasure when she realized not a single one of them was looking out at her with anything approaching a smile on their faces.

She froze beside Luca, who already had his hand on the door.

"What did you tell them?" she asked.

"My people?" He sounded far too triumphant, mixed in with that usual hint of laziness that she was beginning to suspect was all for show. "The truth, of course."

"And which truth is that?"

"There is only the one," Luca said. Happily, she thought. Again. "My father's petulant trophy wife has insisted she be given a job she does not deserve. We do not have jobs hanging about without anyone to fill them, so there was some reshuffling required."

"I assumed you'd be giving me janitorial duties." She arched a brow at him. "Wasn't the idea to make sure this was as unpleasant for me as possible?"

"I made you my executive assistant," Luca replied smoothly, his dark eyes glittering. "It is the most coveted position in this branch of the company." He shifted back slightly. Relaxing, she realized. Because he was obviously enjoying himself. That sent a shiver of ice straight down her spine. So did his smile—which she was close enough to see did not reach his eyes. "It is second only to me, you see. That's quite a bit of power to wield."

She frowned at him. "Why would you do that? Why not make me file things in some basement?"

"Because, *Stepmother*," Luca said in that slow, dark way of his that should not have gotten tangled up in all her breathless memories of that kiss, not when it was clearly meant to be a blow, "that would only delay the inevitable. I am quite certain you won't make it the allocated three years. But if you leave after three days? Three weeks? All the better."

She stiffened. "I won't leave."

He nodded toward the group of people inside, all eyeing her with ill-disguised hostility.

"Each and every person in that room was handpicked by me. They earned their positions here. They function together as a tight and usually congenial team. But I have informed them that all of that is a thing of the past, as you must be shoehorned in whether we like it or not." He turned his gaze on her. "As you can see, they're thrilled."

Kathryn's stomach sank to her feet, because she understood what he'd done. Her pathetic little fantasies of distinguishing herself somehow through hard work in some forgotten corner of the office where she could quietly shine crumbled all around her.

Her mother would be furious. She'd claim that this was exactly what had happened when Kathryn tried to defy her and strike out on her own. Kathryn felt a sinking feeling in her gut, as if maybe Rose was right.

And maybe it was hideously disloyal, maybe it made her a terrible person and an ungrateful child, but Kathryn really, really didn't want that to be true.

"You painted a target on my back," she said now, her lips feeling numb. "You did it deliberately."

This time, Luca's smile reached his eyes, but that didn't make it any warmer. Or this situation any better. "I did."

Then he pushed open the conference room door and fed her straight to the wolves.

CHAPTER FOUR

THREE HARD WEEKS and two days later, Kathryn boarded the Castelli family private jet on the airfield outside Rome, this time in her capacity as the most hated employee in Luca's office. She marched up the folded-down stairs with her back straight and her head high—because that title, of course, was an upgrade compared to her previous role as the most hated stepmother in Castelli family history.

She thought she had this being-loathed thing under control.

It was all about the smile.

Kathryn smiled every time conversation halted abruptly when she entered a room. She smiled when her coworkers pretended they didn't understand her and made her repeat her question once, then twice, so she'd feel foolish as her words hung there in the air between them. She smiled when she was ignored in meetings. She smiled when she was called on to answer questions about past projects she couldn't possibly know anything about. She smiled when Luca berated her for allowing unrestricted access to him and she smiled brighter when he let his people in and out the side door of his office himself, so he could do it all over again.

She smiled and she smiled. The benefit of having been splashed across a thousand tabloids and held to be *so good* and *so self-sacrificing* was that she found she could use *Saint Kate* as a guide through each and every one of her chilly office interactions. Especially because she was well aware that the less she reacted, the more it annoyed her coworkers.

Luca, of course, was a different issue altogether.

She ducked into the plane and made her way into the upgraded living room space, smiling serenely as she took her seat on the curved leather sofa that commanded the center of the room. Luca was already sprawled out at one of the tables to the side that seated three apiece in luxurious leather armchairs, one hand in his hair as usual and the other clamping his mobile to his ear.

He eyed her as he finished his conversation in low Italian, and didn't stop when it was done.

"You're still here," he said. Eventually.

She smiled brighter. "Of course. I told you I wouldn't leave."

"You can't possibly have enjoyed these past few weeks, Kathryn."

"You certainly went out of your way to make sure of that," she agreed. She showed him her teeth. "Much appreciated."

He frowned, and she smiled, and that went on for so long, she was tempted to turn on the big-screen television and ignore him—but that was not how an employee would behave, she imagined.

"You were at the office when I arrived this morning," he said gruffly.

"Every morning."

"I beg your pardon?"

"I'm at the office when you arrive *every* morning," Kathryn said mildly. "Your assistant can't be late the way I was that first day, can she? It sends the wrong message."

She didn't expect him to admit that he'd deliberately kept her waiting that day, simply so he could chastise her for tardiness. He didn't disappoint her, though there was a gleam she didn't quite understand in his dark eyes as they remained level on hers.

"Surely you have other things to do with your time." He waved a hand at her, as if she was displaying herself in a tiny string bikini rather than wearing another perfectly unobjectionable blouse and skirt, chosen specifically to blend in with everyone else and be unworthy of comment. "Trips to the places rich men frequent, the better to identify your next target, for example."

"I had that all planned for this weekend, of course," she said in her sweetest, most professional tone, "but then you scheduled this trip to California. I guess the gold digging will have to wait."

He didn't speak to her again until the plane reached its cruising altitude and the single, deferential air steward had set out trays of food for their dinner on the dark wood coffee table that sprawled in the center of the jet's deeply comfortable and faintly decadent living room. Kathryn's stomach rumbled at her, reminding her that she'd worked through lunch. And breakfast, for that matter, not that her dedication ever seemed to make a difference in Luca's slippery slope of an office, where she literally could do no right.

You're used to that, aren't you? a voice inside her asked—but she shoved it away. Her mother's disappointment in her hurt, yes, but it wasn't invalid. Kathryn was well aware of her own deficiencies, and not only because she'd heard about them so often.

If she hadn't been so deficient, she reminded herself, she wouldn't have found marrying Gianni to be such a perfect option for her. She'd have excelled at her MBA the way she'd been supposed to do.

"Tell me the story," Luca said after they'd eaten in silence for a while, surprising her.

He had a plate on the table before him and was lounging in his leather armchair as he picked languidly at it, but his seeming nonchalance didn't make her heart beat any slower. Nor did it help matters that they were trapped in a plane together, and Kathryn couldn't seem to make herself think about anything but that. All the gilt edges and wood accents and noncommercial setup and decor in the world couldn't change the fact that she and Luca were suspended above the Atlantic Ocean in the dark, with no buffer between them.

Alone.

That hit her like a punch then slid down deep into her belly and pulsed there, as worrying as it was entirely too hot.

She had never actually been alone with Luca before.

There had always been someone else around. Always. Gianni. Some other member of the Castelli family. Staff. All the people in his office, especially because they all lived to catch her out in a misstep as she muddled her way through her first weeks on the job. Rafael and his family the week of the funeral, never more than a room or two away, liable to walk in at any moment.

This was the first time in over two years that it had ever been just the two of them.

There's a pilot, she told herself as her heart slowed, then beat too hard against her ribs. *You're not* really *alone*.

But she knew even as she thought it that it didn't mean anything. Neither the pilot nor the air steward would disturb Luca unless he summoned them himself. She might as well have stranded herself on a desert island with the man.

That, she reflected helplessly, her mind suddenly full of images of a half-naked Luca gleaming beneath some far-off tropical sun, *is not a helpful line of thought*.

And there was a certain hunger in that dark gaze of his that made her think he was entertaining the same rush of images that she was.

"What story?" she asked, and hated how insubstantial her voice was. And the way his dark gaze sharpened at the sound, as if he knew why.

"The lovely and touching fairy tale of how an obviously virtuous young woman like yourself fell passionately in love with a man who could easily have fathered your parents, of course. What else?"

That was meant to insult her, Kathryn knew. But he'd never asked her that before. No one had. The entire world thought they knew exactly why a younger woman had married a much older man—and that wasn't entirely untrue, of course. There were reasons, and some of those reasons were financial. But that didn't mean it had been as cold or as calculated as Luca was determined to believe.

"It wasn't a fairy tale," she told him, tucking her feet up beneath her on the butter-soft leather sofa and smoothing the edges of her skirt down farther toward her knees. She frowned at him. "It was just...nice. I met him very much by accident at a facility that caters to seniors and people with degenerative health challenges."

He didn't *quite* snort at that. "How touching."

"Surely you know that your father wasn't well, Luca." She shrugged. "He was visiting a specialist. I was in the waiting area and we got to talking."

"You were there, one assumes, to gather some extra polish for your halo and crow about it to the tabloids?"

Kathryn thought of her mother, and the way her body had betrayed her, growing so old and knotted before her time. She thought of the gnarled hands that had scrubbed floors to give Kathryn every possible chance—*I had plans for my life, Kathryn*, Rose had always said in that sharp way of hers, *but I put them aside for you.*

How could Kathryn do anything less than the same in return for her?

"Something like that," she said now, to this man who didn't deserve to know anything about her mother or her struggles, or the choices Kathryn had made to honor the sacrifices that had been made for her, no matter how badly she'd done at that sometimes. "I do so prefer it when my halo shines, you know."

Luca laughed—and it was *that* laugh. That famous spill of light and life and perfection, illuminating his face and making the air between them dance and shimmer for a long, taut moment before he stopped himself, as if he hadn't realized what was happening.

But she could hoard it anyway, Kathryn thought, feeling dazed. She could hold it close. An unexpected gift she could take out and warm herself with during her next sleepless night—and this was not the time to ask herself why she thought anything this man did was a gift. Not when she knew he'd hate her even more for thinking such a thing.

"And a driving, inescapable passion for a septuagenarian overtook you in this waiting area?" he asked, his voice darker than before, his gaze much too shrewd. "I hear that happens. Though not often to young women in their twenties, unless, of course, you were discussing his net worth."

"I liked him," Kathryn said, and that was the truth about her marriage, no matter the extenuating circumstances. She shrugged. "He made me laugh and I made him laugh, too. It wasn't seedy or mercenary, Luca, no matter how much you wish that it was. He was a good friend to me."

A better friend than most, if she was honest.

"A good friend."

"Yes."

"My father. Gianni Castelli. *A good friend*."

Kathryn sighed, and set her plate down on the coffee table, her appetite gone. "I take it you've decided in your infinite wisdom that this, too, must be impossible."

Luca's laugh this time was no gift. Not one anyone in her right mind would want anyway.

"My father was born into wealth, and his single goal was to expand it," he told her harshly, the Italian inflection in his voice stronger than usual. "That was his art and his calling, and he dedicated himself to it with single-minded purpose from the time he could walk. His favorite hobby was marriage—the more inappropriate, the better. Do not beat yourself up. Most of his wives misunderstood the breakdown of his affections and attention."

"I don't think you knew your father very well," Kathryn suggested. She lifted up her hands when Luca's eyes blazed. "Not in the way I did. That's all I mean."

"You're speaking of the two years of your acquaintance with him, as opposed to the whole of my life?"

"A son can't possibly know the man his father was." She lifted a shoulder then dropped it. "He can only know what kind of father he was or wasn't, and piece together what clues he can about the man from that. Isn't that the history of the world? No one ever knows their parents. Not really."

She certainly didn't know hers. Her father had buggered off before she was born, and her mother had given up everything that had mattered to her so Kathryn wouldn't have to bear the weight of that. Kathryn knew the sacrifice. Her mother reminded her of what she'd left behind for Kathryn's sake at every opportunity, and fair enough. But she still couldn't say she understood the woman—much less the way she'd treated Kathryn all her life.

A muscle leaped in Luca's lean jaw.

"I knew my father a great deal longer than you did," he gritted out after a moment. "He had no friends, Kathryn. He had business associates and a collection of wives. Everyone in his life was accorded a role and expected to play it, and woe betide the fool who did not live up to his expectations."

"Is that what this has been about all this time? All the hatred and the nastiness and the threats and so on?" she asked. She tilted her head to one side and said the thing she knew she shouldn't. But she couldn't seem to stop herself. "You...have daddy issues?"

The crack of his temper was very nearly audible. If the plane itself had been thrown off course and sent into a spiraling nosedive toward the ocean, she wouldn't have been at all surprised—and it took Kathryn a long, tense, shuddering moment to understand that the jet they sat on was fine. The plane flew on, unaffected by the minor explosion that had taken over the cabin—and the aftershocks that were still rolling through her.

The only steep and terrible free fall was in her stomach as it plummeted to her feet.

Luca hadn't moved. It only felt as if he had.

She watched, as fascinated as she was alarmed, as he tamped that bright current of fury down. He still didn't move. He stared back at her as if he'd very much like to throttle her. One hand twitched as if he'd considered it. This suggested to her that she'd been more on target than she'd imagined when she'd said it.

But then he blinked and the crisis passed. There was only the usual force of his dislike staring back at her. That and the leftover adrenaline trickling through her veins, making her shift against the sofa cushions.

"Why me?" he asked, his dark voice a spiked thing as it slammed into her. "I've made no secret of my opinion of you. What sort of masochism led you to throw yourself in my path when you must know you'd have had a much better time in another branch of the company?"

"Is that a thinly veiled way of asking if I'm pursuing you for my usual gold-digging ends?" she asked, unable to tear her gaze from his and equally unsure why that was. Why did he *invade* her like this? Why did she feel as if he had more control over her than she did?

"Was it veiled, thinly or otherwise?" he asked, his voice soft. If no less harsh. "I must be doing it wrong."

Kathryn's smile felt forced, but she didn't let it fade. She had the wild notion, suddenly, that it was all she had.

"I considered working for your brother, of course," she said quietly. "I doubt he's particularly fond of me, but there's certainly none of...this." She waved her hand between them, in that too-thick air and that taut electric storm that charged it. "It would have been easier, certainly."

"Then, why?" Luca's mouth curled into something much too dark to be any kind of smile, and the echo of it pulsed inside her. "To punish us both?"

"The fact is that your brother maintains the business and he's very good at it," Kathryn said. "He will make certain the Castelli name endures, that no ground will be lost on his watch. He's a very steady hand on the wheel."

"And I am what?" Luca didn't quite laugh. "The drunken driver in this scenario? I drive too fast, Kathryn. But never drunk."

"You're the innovator," she said quietly. It felt... dangerous to praise him to his face. To do something other than suffer through his darkness. "You're the creative force in the company. Never satisfied. Always pushing a new boundary." She shrugged, more uncomfortable than she could remember ever having been around him before, and that was saying something. "My personal feelings about you aside, there's no more exciting place to work. You must know this. I assume that's why all your employees are so—" Kathryn smiled that little bit brighter, and that, too, was harder than it should have been "—fiercely protective."

Luca looked thrown, which she might have considered a victory at any other time—but there was something about the way he gazed at her then. It seemed to sneak into her, wrapping itself around her bones and drawing tight. Too tight.

"Can you do that?" he asked, his voice mild but with that *something* beneath it. "Put your personal feelings aside?"

She met his gaze. She didn't flinch.

"I have to if I want this job to mean something," Kathryn told him, aware as she spoke that this might have been the most honest she'd ever been with him. As if she had nothing to lose, when that couldn't be further from the truth. This was her only chance to prove that she could make something of herself without her mother's input or directives. This was her only chance to honor her mother's sacrifices—and also stay free. "And I do. Unlike you, I don't have a choice."

The Castelli château, the center of Castelli Wine's operations in the States, perched at the top of Northern California's fertile Sonoma Valley like a particularly self-satisfied grande dame. The vineyards stretched out much like voluminous queenly skirts, rolling out over the hills in all directions, seeming to take over this part of the valley all the way to the horizon and back. Tonight the winery gleamed prettily through the crisp winter night, bright lights in every window as a line of cars snaked down the long drive between the marching rows of cypress trees.

Luca loved the unapologetic spectacle of it—the high Italianate drama in every detail, from the epic sweep of the house itself to the grounds kept in a condition to rival the Boboli Gardens in Florence, delighting the tourists on their wine-tasting tours of Sonoma—despite himself.

Tonight was the annual Castelli Wine Winter Ball. This was the reason Luca had flown across the world, landing only a scant hour earlier, which he was sure Rafael would think was cutting it a bit close. He and Rafael needed to make it abundantly clear to all and sundry that nothing had changed since Gianni's passing. That everything was business as usual at Castelli Wine.

And as with most things in life, the more elegant and relaxed and attractive the face of a thing, the more people were likely to believe it.

Kathryn, Luca thought grimly, certainly proved that rule. And so did he. He banked on it, in fact.

He checked his watch for the fifth time in as many seconds, unreasonably irritated that she hadn't been waiting for him when he'd emerged from his bedroom suite, showered and dressed and as recovered from their flight as it was possible to be in such a short time. He could already hear the band in the great ballroom and the sound of very well-heeled enjoyment below, all clinking glasses and graceful laughter, wafting up into the far reaches of the family wing and down the long hall to this remote set of rooms set apart from the rest.

Luca glared at Kathryn's door, as if that might make her appear.

And when it did—when it started to open as if he'd commanded it with that glare—he scowled even more.

Until she stepped out into the hall, and then, he was fairly certain, all the blood in his head sank with an audible thud to his sex.

"What—" and his voice was a strangled version of

his own, even from the great distance that ringing in his ears made it sound "—*the hell* are you wearing?"

Kathryn eyed him with that cool expression of hers that he was beginning to think might be the death of him. It clawed at him. It made him want nothing more than to heat her up and see what lurked beneath it.

"I believe it's called a dress," she said crisply.

"No."

She stood there a moment. Blinked. "No? Are you sure? The last time I checked a dictionary, the word was definitely *dress*. Or perhaps *gown*? A case could be made for each, though I think—"

"Be quiet."

Her mouth snapped closed and she had no idea how lucky she was that he hadn't silenced her in the way he'd much prefer. He could already taste her again, as if he had. Luca pushed off the wall opposite her door, unable to control himself. Unable to *think*.

A red haze of sheer lust kicked through him, making everything else dim.

Yes, Kathryn was wearing a dress. Barely. It was in an off-white shade that should have made her look like a ghost, with that English complexion of hers, but instead made her seem to glow. As if she'd been lit from within by a buttery shimmer. It had a delicate, high neckline and no sleeves, and an elegant sort of wide belt that wrapped around her waist before the full skirt cascaded all the way to the floor.

None of that was the problem. *That* could have been Grace Kelly, it was all so effortlessly tasteful and stylish.

It was the damned cutouts that made his entire body feel like a single, taut ache. Two huge wedges that edged in at sharp angles from the sides, cutting into the lower bodice of the dress and showing sheer acres of her bare skin in that sweet spot below her breasts and above her navel, then flaring out over the curves of her sides.

Luca wanted to taste her everywhere he saw skin. Right here. Right now.

He didn't realize he'd said that out loud until her eyes went wide and turned that fascinating slate-green shade, and then it didn't matter anyway, because he'd lost his mind—and worse, his control. He backed her into her own closed door, bracing himself over her with a hand on either side of her head.

"You can't," Kathryn said. *Whispered*, more like, her voice a rough little scrape that he could feel in the hardest part of him. "Luca. We *can't.*"

Luca didn't ask himself what he was doing. He didn't care. That dress pooled around her, seductive and impossible, and he was lost in the elegant line of her neck and the hair she'd swept back into a complicated chignon at her nape.

"Did my father give you these diamonds?" he asked, trying to force this red-hazed lust out of him by any means possible. But it didn't shift at all, not even when he lifted a finger to trace the sparkling stones she wore in both her ears. One, then the next.

All of this was wrong. That pounding ache in his sex. This impossible hunger that stormed through him, casting everything else aside—including his own good intentions. He knew it. He still couldn't seem to care about that as he should. As he knew he would eventually.

"Answer me," he urged her, his mouth much too close to the sweet temptation of that tender spot behind her ear, and he couldn't identify that dark, driving thing that had control of him then. "What did you have to do to earn them, Kathryn?"

She jerked her head to the side, away from his fingers and the way they toyed with the delicate shell of her ear, but it was too late. He could see the way she shivered. He could see the pulse that fluttered madly in her neck. He could see the goose bumps that ran down her bare arms.

There was no ordering himself to pretend he hadn't seen those things. Or that he didn't know what they meant.

"You are meant to be here as my assistant, nothing more," he reminded her, his voice a low throb in the otherwise quiet hallway. "This is not meant to be an opportunity for you to flaunt your wares and pick up new customers."

"You're disgusting."

The icy condemnation in her voice poured over him, gas to a flame.

"That is an interesting choice of words," Luca murmured, his lips the barest breath away from her warm neck, and she shuddered. "What is more disgusting, do you think—the fact that I do not want you parading around the château, contaminating my family home and my father's memory? Or the fact you have no qualms about wearing a dress that makes every man in the vicinity think of nothing but you, naked?"

She turned her head to face him then, and her hands came up, shoving futilely at his chest. Luca didn't budge, and he had the distinct pleasure—or was it pain, he couldn't tell—of watching the color rise in her exquisite cheeks.

"Only you think that," she snapped at him, mutiny

and feminine awareness and something hotter by far in her furious gaze. "Because only you live your life with your head in the gutter. Everyone else will see a lovely dress by a well-known designer and nothing more."

"They will see my father's widow in white, with her naked body on display," he corrected her. "They will see your complete disregard for propriety, to say nothing of the memory of your very dear *friend*."

She laughed. It was a high, outraged sound.

"What should I have worn instead?" she demanded. "A black shroud? What would make you happy, Luca? A tent of shame?"

His hands shook and he flattened them against the wall, because he knew. *He knew.* If he touched her again, he wouldn't stop. He didn't care how much more he'd hate himself for it.

He wasn't sure he'd even try to stop himself.

"You told me your laughable story," he reminded her. "An unlikely friendship struck by chance in a far-off waiting room, between one of the wealthiest men in the world and you, our favorite saint." He studied the way her lush mouth firmed at that, the way her eyes flashed and darkened. "I think I saw the syrupy cable-television movie you based that absurd nursery rhyme on. What is the real story, I wonder?"

"I can't help it if you're so cynical and so jaded that all you see in the world is what you put into it," she threw at him with something more than mere temper in her eyes—and it fascinated him. That was his curse. *She* fascinated him, damn her. Maybe she had from the start. Maybe that was the truth he'd been burying for two years. "Here's a news flash, Luca. If you spend your life looking for ulterior motives and cruelty, that's all you'll ever see. It's a self-fulfilling prophecy."

"Do you know why I hate you, Kathryn?" He didn't wait for her answer. "It's not that you married my father for his money. So did everyone else. It's that you dare to act offended when anyone calls that spade the spade it is. It's that you believe your own tabloid coverage. *Saint Kate* is a myth. You are nothing like a saint at all."

She made a frustrated sound and shoved at him again. "I can't control what you think of me. I certainly can't control what the tabloids say about me. And this might come as a giant shock to you, but I don't *care* if you hate me or not."

Somehow he didn't believe her, and he couldn't have said why that was.

And something inside him cracked. A chain broke, and he shifted, leaning in closer and then reaching down to trace the cutout angle of her dress that was closest to him. He sketched his way from the tender skin at the juncture of her shoulder and chest down, skating around the tempting swell of her breast, then cutting in with the line of the fabric toward her belly.

Her breath came hard. Broken.

But she didn't tell him to stop. She didn't shove at him again. Her hands curled into fists and rested there against his lapels, urging him on.

Luca concentrated on the task of this. Of his fingertip against her insane, impossible smoothness. Of the fire that danced between them, the flames stretching ever higher, until he was wrapped up in the sensation of her skin beneath his and the scent of her besides. The hint of something tropical in her hair and the subtle, powdery notes that whispered of the very expensive perfume he now associated with her so strongly that the hint of it in places she wasn't made his body clench down hard in awareness.

Once in a distant resort in the Austrian Alps. Once in a seaside hotel in the Bahamas. She hadn't been in either place, but she was here. Tonight, she was here.

And this was no different. *This is madness*, he told himself.

He didn't kiss her. He didn't dare risk the possibility that he wouldn't stop this time. But he leaned in closer anyway, until their breaths were the same breath. Until he could see every last thing she felt as it moved through her expressive eyes. Until the fact he *wasn't* taking that mouth with his, that their only point of contact was his finger as it danced along that edge where fabric met skin, became erotic.

It became everything.

And he wanted this too much. He wanted *her.* Luca wanted to lose himself inside her, to hurl them both straight into the heart of this wildfire that was eating them both alive.

"This," he said softly, "is what a whore wears when she wishes to announce she's available again. Discreetly, I grant you. But the message is the same."

He felt the way she stiffened, and then he indulged himself and wrapped the whole of his palm over the exposed indentation of her waist, and, God help him, the smooth heat of her blasted into him. It ricocheted inside him. It lit him on fire.

It made that hunger in him shift from an insistent pulse to a roar.

But even though he could feel the deep, low shudders that moved through her body, that told him she felt the same need that he did, she shoved at him again. Much harder this time, using her fists. He grunted and backed up.

He didn't remove his hand.

"What's your plan, Luca?" Her gaze was dark, and he couldn't read her. Her chin edged higher, and her voice was cool and hard. That was what penetrated the red haze, like shards of ice deep into him. "Are you going to prove I'm a whore by acting like one yourself? Do you think that's how it's done?"

Luca dropped his hand then, with far more reluctance than he cared to examine just then. He stood away from her, lust and longing and that greedy kick of need making him scowl at her. Making him wish too many things he shouldn't.

Making him wonder why she was the only thing he couldn't seem to control—or, more to the point, his reaction to her.

"I don't need to prove the truth," he gritted out. What the hell was happening to him? How had she gotten the better of his control? He tried to shake it off. "It simply is, no matter how you pad it out and pretend otherwise to make yourself look better."

She straightened, only that flush high on her cheeks and the hectic glitter in her too-dark eyes to mark what had happened here.

What had *almost* happened.

"I think you'll find that math doesn't work," Kathryn said crisply, and she might as well have shoved a knife deep into his side. He felt as if she had. "Whorish behavior always adds up to two whores, Luca. Not one dirty whore and an innocent with dirty hands by accident, almost but not quite corrupted by doing the exact same thing. No matter what lies you tell yourself."

And then she pushed past him and started down the hall, her every movement as graceful and elegant as if she was a damned queen, not the grasping little gold digger they both knew full well she was.

CHAPTER FIVE

THE PARTY WAS long and bright and painful.

Of course, it always had been. Kathryn told herself that, really, this was no different than the other times she'd had to parade around the Castelli château in this gorgeous little pocket of the Northern California wine country, acting as if she neither heard nor saw the whispers and the overlong, unpleasantly speculative looks.

This was merely part and parcel of being notorious, she told herself. Something every other member of the Castelli family had found a way to handle. Why couldn't she do the same?

But, of course, she knew.

It was Luca. At every other party she'd ever been to with him, he'd kept as much distance between them as possible, as if he feared too much proximity to her would contaminate him. But this time she was his assistant, no longer his stepmother. That meant her place was at his elbow, no matter what had happened between them in that hallway.

And worse, what had *almost* happened. What she told herself she absolutely would not have allowed to happen—but she could feel the hollowness of that assertion tying her stomach into knots.

He'd caught up to her on the stairs that led down toward the ballroom and had slid a dark, fulminating look her way as he'd fallen into place beside her.

"I think you should leave me alone," she'd told him. Through her teeth.

"With pleasure," he'd replied silkily. "Does this mean you quit?"

She'd glared at him, and he'd caught her by the arm when she'd very nearly missed a step, and then held her fast when she would have yanked herself away from him.

"Careful," he'd warned her. "We are no longer in private. And in public, you are my father's widow and my current assistant."

"That is, in fact, all I am anywhere." She'd shaken her head at him. "Except for the sewer inside your head, of course."

"One scandal at a time," he'd told her, sounding something very much like *grim.* He'd let her go when they'd reached the ground floor. "Tonight I think the fact the Widow Castelli has joined the workforce will have to carry the gossip news cycle, don't you? Unless you'd like to use this opportunity to update your global dating profile by announcing to the world that your hunt for a protector has begun anew."

"And by *hunt*," she'd retorted icily, "am I to understand you mean something like you manhandling me in a hallway? Was that your version of an audition?"

Luca's mouth had curved in that lethal way that was nothing so palatable as a smile.

"It's a tragedy for you that you can't manipulate me, I'm sure," he'd said, sounding anything but tragic. "Make sure you schedule time in my calendar for me to

care about that. Maybe next month? In the meantime—"
and he'd switched then, from the obnoxious Luca she'd
come to expect into the COO version of Luca that she'd
only ever seen in action over the past few weeks in his
office "—you stay next to me. You do not speak unless
spoken to directly. Just smile and look pretty and make
sure you remember every detail of every conversation
we have so we can compare notes later."

She'd blinked. "Uh, what details am I looking for?"

He'd stared down at her, and it was getting harder
and harder for her to imagine how anyone saw him as
a lazy, lackadaisical playboy when the truth of him
was stark and obvious and stamped right there on his
intensely beautiful face.

"All of them, Kathryn," he said, as if she was an
idiot. She hated that he made her feel like one—and si-
multaneously feel as if she needed to prove him wrong.
Then again, she'd had a great deal of experience with
that feeling. "You never know which little detail will
make all the difference."

And then he'd strode ahead of her straight into the
ballroom, and the moment he'd entered it, become that
other Luca. As if he'd flipped a switch.

Affable and approachable. Quick to make everyone
around him laugh. He always had a drink in his hand
and appeared to be ever so slightly tipsy, though this
close to him, Kathryn discovered that he didn't actually drink much. He slapped backs and kissed cheeks.
He flirted with everybody. He was delightful and about
as unthreatening as a man who looked like him and
moved like him and wore black tie as easily as he did
ever could.

Kathryn didn't have to ask him why he bothered to

put on such an elaborate act. The *why* of it became clear almost instantly.

She'd spent a great deal of time smiling prettily next to Gianni, too, and no one had found him particularly delightful. They'd always been guarded. Distant and cagey. Especially if they were somehow involved in the business.

But it was as if no one could believe that *this* Luca Castelli, who commanded the attention of the whole party simply by entering it, was the same one who ran the Rome office with such a deft hand. This bright, gleaming, careless creature. Even though there was no other name on that door in Rome but his.

Kathryn had heard the rumors. That it was Gianni himself who'd propped up Luca's office—except, of course, for the small problem that an old man with dementia could not possibly have run anything. Perhaps he simply had a particularly good team to support him, the rumor mill had countered. But no matter what people speculated about in private, when they were in Luca's presence, they basked in it. In him. In that effortless sort of sunshine he spread about him so easily.

And they told him everything.

Secrets. Rumors. Things their supervisors—who were often standing across the room—would kill them for saying out loud.

Everyone succumbed to the golden myth of Luca Castelli, Kathryn saw. Everyone. Captains of industry, wine connoisseurs and college-age caterers alike lost in the perfection of his inviting smile.

Watching him in action told her a great many things, but most of all, it made her feel better about herself for falling so completely under his spell every time he got too close to her. It wasn't something fatal in her own design, as she'd imagined. It wasn't that weakness in her that her mother had always despaired of and had gone to such lengths to stamp out of her. It was *him*.

She ducked into the mostly hidden powder room off the main ballroom when Luca got into an intense discussion about a documentary Kathryn had never seen with a handful of very intellectual types who'd made it clear they both recognized her and thought her beneath them. *Far* beneath them. She was happy to let them think so.

Inside the luxurious bathroom suite, she sat down on the couch in the lounge area and took a little breather. Away from the crush of the crowd, most of whom looked at her with nothing but ugly supposition on their faces. Away from Luca, whom she really should hate.

Why didn't she hate him the way she should? The way he unapologetically hated her?

"Being fascinated with him is only making everything worse," she snapped at herself, out loud—and then jumped when the door to the lounge swung open.

"Oh," Lily said. She looked around as if she expected there to be more people in the room—or as if she'd heard Kathryn talking to herself like a crazy person. Kathryn trotted out her smile automatically. "I didn't realize anyone was in here."

"Only me," Kathryn said mildly. "Depending on your point of view, that may or may not count."

Rafael's wife laughed, then smoothed her hands over the swell of her pregnant belly, looking resplendent in a gleaming blue gown. And happy. That it took her a moment to recognize what that expression meant made something inside Kathryn catch. As if happiness was so foreign to her.

"Don't pay any attention to Luca," Lily said, her eyes meeting Kathryn's in the mirror then moving away. "The man is *such* a control freak. He can't stand surprises, that's all."

She ran the water in the sink and then smoothed her damp palms over the coils of heavy braids she wore, all collected into a fat bun at the back of her head. Kathryn had always liked Lily. She was the least judgmental member of the Castelli family. She'd been the most welcoming to Kathryn, and Kathryn had even imagined that under different circumstances they might have been friends. Perhaps that, too, was naive.

She was beginning to realize that *she* was naive, in every possible way—something she'd have thought was impossible, given how hard her mother had worked to wring that out of her. And yet.

"Am I a surprise?" she asked, when she was sure she could keep her voice light and easy. "I don't think that's the word Luca would use."

Lily slanted an amused look at her. "Everything about you is a surprise," she said. "From the day you arrived. You refuse to slot yourself into one of Luca's depressingly functional and supernaturally clean boxes. He hates that."

"He hates surprises?" Kathryn laughed lightly. Very lightly, which was at odds with how her heart punched at her, as if this information about Luca was the most important detail of all she might have collected here tonight. "Here I thought the only thing he hated was me."

It was Lily's turn to laugh, though hers seemed far less for show.

"He hates messes," she said. "He always has. If he hates you? It's because you're messing things up for him, and he doesn't know how to handle something he can't sanitize and shelve somewhere. And between you and me, that's probably a good thing."

Then she smiled her goodbyes and went back out into the crush, leaving Kathryn to mull that over.

But not for long. Her mobile buzzed in her clutch and she knew it was Luca, which got her moving out of the bathroom lounge and back into the party before she even looked at the display.

"Are you taking a holiday?" he growled into the phone when she answered, all spleen and fury. "If not, you'd better be right here when I turn around. I'm not paying you to gallivant around the château like one of the guests."

"Are you paying me at all?" she asked mildly, spotting him several groups away and moving around them as she spoke. "I thought your father set up a trust for me so you couldn't hold a paycheck over my head. Or maybe for other reasons, and that's just a happy accident?"

"I'm turning around now," he said, and she came to a stop before him as he did.

Their eyes met. Held.

It was harder than it should have been to pull herself away. To concentrate on tucking her mobile back in her clutch. To tell herself there was nothing at all in his dark eyes but what there always was: some or other form of fury, brightened up with dislike.

She didn't understand why no one could see the truth about him but her. She told herself she was making it up. That it wouldn't be there when she looked up at him again—that he'd be that half lazy, half obnoxious man he should have been and nothing more.

But it was still there. That fury, that need. That hunger that terrified her and intrigued her in equal measure. A whole world in that gaze of his, and she had no earthly idea what to do about it.

"I think you're being paged," she told him, nodding toward a bejeweled woman in a slinky dress made entirely of sequins, who was bearing down on Luca from afar. "You wouldn't want to disappoint your fans with this show of seriousness, would you?"

"It's not a show. It's business. Not a concept I expect you to comprehend."

"I'm sure that's what you tell yourself," she said unwisely. So very unwisely. "But it's interesting that you're so determined to hide part of yourself away wherever you go, don't you think?"

She had no idea why she'd said that. Luca looked frozen into place for a long, taut moment, an arrested expression on his darkly gorgeous face. Then he blinked, and there was nothing but his usual darkness again, leaving Kathryn faintly dizzy.

"Careful, Stepmother," he said softly. Lethally. "Or I might be tempted to truly give them something to talk about tonight."

She didn't believe he'd do anything of the kind—of course she didn't—but she still had to fight to restrain a shiver at the thought. And she was sure that Luca knew it, that the unholy gleam of something like gold in his dark eyes was that pure male knowledge Kathryn was very much afraid would be her undoing.

But then he turned away, his public smile at the ready, that intensity gone as if it had never been.

And Kathryn reminded herself that it didn't matter what this man's sister-in-law, who had once been his stepsister, had said in the bathroom lounge. It didn't matter what happened in remote hallways in the château. The only truth that mattered was that she was his assistant now, and if she couldn't do that job as well as she should, everything else he'd ever said about her was true. And not just him.

You've had more opportunities than I could have dreamed of having! her mother had said the last time she'd seen her, at Christmas, with that look on her face that had told Kathryn that once again she'd failed Rose terribly, as she'd always managed to do. "And look what you've done with them."

Kathryn hadn't known what to say or how to defend herself. Because Rose had been the one to encourage Kathryn into marrying Gianni in the first place.

"The world is filled with people who marry for far less reason than this," she'd said. "But of course, Kathryn, it's *your* life. You should do what you think is best *for you*, no matter who else might benefit."

And Kathryn hadn't been able to think of a good reason why *not* to marry the kindly old man when her mother had put it like that—especially given what she knew she would gain from it. It would cost her so very little. All *she* had to sacrifice was a couple of years. Not her whole life, as her mother had done, and for far less in return. Though Rose certainly hadn't objected when Gianni's money had allowed Kathryn to buy her a cottage in the sweet Yorkshire village of her choice, and then provide her with live-in care.

She never thanked you, either, a little voice pointed out, deep inside her.

But she felt ungrateful and small even thinking such things. Many women wouldn't have had a baby on their own, with the father adamantly out of the picture. Rose had never faltered.

Which meant Kathryn could do no less—no matter the provocation.

It was time she stopped worrying about Luca Castelli and what he thought about her, and got to work.

One blue-and-gold California day rolled into the next, filled with meetings and vineyard tours and endless business dinners, and Luca found himself more disgruntled than he should have been by the fact Kathryn was…good at the job. More than good, in fact, in the odd role she had to play. Far better at it than the assistant she'd displaced, though he hated to admit it. Marco had been an excellent administrative assistant, but had always been a little too conspicuously himself when out in the field trying to charm potential clients.

Kathryn, on the other hand—who Luca would have asserted could no more *blend* than the sun could rise in the west and was anything but charming besides— did it beautifully.

"No," he barked out one morning, when she'd walked into their shared breakfast room dressed in one of her usual work outfits, a skirt and heels and one of those soft blouses that made him unable to think of anything at all but the breasts pressed *just there* behind the silk.

Kathryn paused, her hand on the back of the nearest chair, her bearing that of slightly offended royalty. It put his teeth on edge.

"You can't wear that," he growled at her, feeling like some kind of sulky child, which was insupportable. He was not one of his nephews, having a tantrum. Why couldn't he control himself around this woman? "We are walking through the vines with one of the accounts today. They find the Castelli family on the verge of being too European for their tastes as is, so we must be certain to impress them with our homespun, regular-person charm."

"I don't think even you can convince someone you are either homespun or regular."

"I'm a chameleon," he said drily. And was uncomfortable with how that sat there on the sunny table like truth, when he hadn't meant it that way. *It's interesting that you're so determined to hide part of yourself away wherever you go*, she'd said, damn her. He scowled at her. "But I doubt you can say the same."

He was wrong. Kathryn turned and left the room and when she reappeared, she'd transformed herself. She wore jeans, a pair of boots and a soft, casual, long-sleeved shirt. She'd let her hair down to pool around her shoulders and had scrubbed the makeup from her face. She looked like a host of fantasies he hadn't realized he had. She looked like an advertisement for healthy Californian living. Like a dream come true.

The emissaries from this tricky account of theirs had agreed, hanging on Kathryn's every word and acting as if Luca was *her* assistant, a state of affairs that didn't annoy him as much as it should have done— because he got to trail behind her, admiring the curve of her bottom in faded denim.

And imagining what it would be like to throw her down in one of the tidy rows between the vines and taste all that sweet, soft skin and that mouth that was driving him to the brink of madness.

When they were finally alone again, having waved off the ebullient account managers who'd doubled their national order based entirely on the force of Kathryn's smile, he found himself watching her much too closely. As if he might pounce.

"I told you I could do the job," she said, and he wondered if she knew how fierce she sounded. "Any job."

"So you did."

"But don't worry, Luca," she said, and he had the sense she'd collected herself—remembered who they were. He hated that he felt it as a kind of loss—and it seemed to collect inside him with all the other things he hated about himself. "I won't let that get in the way of all my whoring around. I know you need that to feel better about yourself and, of course, my only aim is to please you."

He felt his jaw clench and every muscle in his body tense. But there was something about the way she stood there in the bright winter sun, her hands tucked into the back pockets of her jeans and the Sonoma wind toying with her dark hair. He had the strangest sense of tightness around his chest, as if there was a steel band clamping down on him.

He didn't know what to do with it. He didn't know how to handle it. Or her.

Or worst of all, himself.

"Why did you marry him?" he asked.

Her marvelous eyes were dove gray in all that too-blue California light, and she didn't look away from him.

"I don't see why it matters to you."

"And yet it does."

"I think you want there to be some kind of rationale,"

she said quietly. "Something you can point to that makes it all okay in your head. Because otherwise you're just a man who has grabbed his father's widow. Twice."

"Is there one, then? A rationale? Were you a street urchin he saved? Did you personally support a threatened orphanage and his money saved a host of children from eviction?"

She smiled at him, and it wasn't her usual smile. It wasn't that serene, bulletproof smile she trotted out for work and had used on him at least a thousand times in the past three weeks alone. This one hurt. It was sad and it was reflected in her eyes, and he didn't understand what was happening here.

What had already happened, if he was honest with himself.

Luca decided honesty was overrated. But it was too late. She was speaking.

"No," she said. "I married him because I wanted to marry him. He was rich and I was struggling through my degree and some personal issues, and he told me he could make all my troubles go away. I liked that. I wanted that." His mouth twisted, but her smile only deepened, and still it hurt. "Is that what you wanted to hear?"

"It doesn't surprise me."

"What do you think marriage is, Luca?" she asked, and she tilted her head slightly to one side.

He was mesmerized by it, by *her*, and it occurred to him that they'd never actually *talked* before. It had been all insults and glares, that scene in the library or in the hallway between their rooms, what he still thought was just another rehearsed story on the plane. She shook her hair back from her face and he wanted to do that for her. He wanted to touch her, he realized, more than he could recall ever wanting anything else.

And nothing had ever been more impossible.

"Not the transaction it was for you," he said, aware that his voice was too raw, too rough. It gave him away. "Not a bit of cold calculation with a monetized end."

But Kathryn only continued to smile at him in that same way, as if *he* made her sad. As if he was *doing something* to her. That tight band around his chest seemed to pull even tauter. It pinched.

"Who are you to judge?" she asked softly, and it was more of a slap, perhaps, because it lacked heat or accusation. She simply asked. "We were happy with our arrangement. We fulfilled the promises we made to each other."

He couldn't take it. He moved toward her, aware but not caring that they were standing out in front of the château where anyone could see them, and he took her face between his hands. This would be so much easier if she weren't so pretty, he told himself—if she was a little more plastic and a whole lot less polished.

If she didn't short-circuit every bit of control he'd ever had.

"Tell me more about how happy you were," he dared her, aware that he was furious. More than furious. "How perfect your marriage was—a union of two identical souls, yes?"

But she didn't back down. She didn't flush hot or look the least bit ashamed. Her hands came up and hooked around his wrists, but she didn't pull him away.

"Go on, then," Luca urged her, his voice an aching thing that simmered in the scant space between them. "Tell me how you fulfilled those promises to the old man. Were you contractually obligated to kneel before him and pleasure him a certain number of nights per week? Or was he past that point—did he have you tend to yourself while he watched? What promises did you keep, Kathryn?"

Something gleamed in that gaze of hers and turned her eyes a darker shade of gray, but she didn't jerk away from him.

"What amazes me about you," she whispered, "is how you think it's your right to ask these questions. You don't get to know what happened in my marriage. You can drive yourself crazy with all your dark imaginings, and I hope you do. You can whisper your filthy thoughts to anyone who will listen. It doesn't make them true, and it certainly doesn't require me to comment on them. If you want to believe that's what happened between me and your father, then go ahead. Believe it."

There was a resolve in her gaze Luca didn't like, and he didn't know what he might have done then, but down at the bottom of the château's long drive, a busload of wine tasters pulled in and started up the winding way toward them.

And he had no choice but to let her go.

Kathryn woke when the moonlight poured in her windows, making her blink in confusion at the clock. It was just before four in the morning, and that was, she realized after a moment or two of uncertainty, very definitely the moon and not the sun.

Her internal clock was still a mess, even after nearly a week in California, and she only had to lie there a little while before she accepted the reality that she was not going to fall back asleep. Not tonight.

She swung her feet over the side of the tall, canopied bed piled high with soft linens, and dressed quickly in the clothes she'd left draped over her chair, a simple pair of terry lounging trousers and a cashmere hooded top. She twisted her hair back out of her way, tying it in a knot at her nape. She wrapped a long merino wool sweater around her to cut the chill, and then she pushed open the glass doors that led out onto her balcony and stepped outside.

The moon was huge and so bright it lit up the whole of the valley and all Kathryn could see in all directions, pouring over the cypress trees and dancing over the gnarled rows of vines. Making the pockets of night where it didn't touch even darker, and turning the world a spectral silver. The breeze was high, whipping into her, just cold enough to feel like exhilaration.

She closed her eyes and leaned into it.

"Couldn't sleep?" asked a low male voice from far too close. "Perhaps it's your conscience."

Kathryn looked over, as slowly as possible, as a counterpoint to the sudden clatter of her heart. She'd forgotten that the balconies of these rooms all ran together here at the far end of the château, despite half walls between the rooms that were little more than decorative gestures toward privacy and did nothing to conceal her from Luca. Nothing at all.

He was sprawled on one of the soft loungers, wearing nothing but a pair of exercise trousers very low on his hips, as if he was impervious to the winter air around him.

And the moonlight crawled all over him. Sliding across that vast expanse of his chest, cavorting in the ridges and hollows, licking him and writhing over him, illuminating every inch of his shocking male beauty. And doing nothing at all to temper that stark expression on his face or that dark hunger in his eyes.

"Says the man who's clearly been out here awhile," Kathryn replied. Lightly. So very lightly. As if he was nothing to her. As if his voice did nothing to her. As if this was as unremarkable as having any other sort of meeting with him in the broad daylight, surrounded by other people.

But it was as if he knew exactly what she was trying to hide, or perhaps the moon showed him far too much, because he made it worse. He stood.

"What are you doing out here?" she asked.

"I have no idea," he said in a low voice, his gaze still on her. "Something I'm certain I'll regret. But that is nothing new."

The clatter of her heart became a deep bass drumming.

Luca raked back that thick fall of hair, the gesture as lazy as his hot eyes were not. Then he started toward her in that low, rolling gait that marked him as exactly the sort of predator she needed most to avoid.

Kathryn knew she shouldn't try to tough this out. She knew that there was no shame at all in simply turning tail and running, barring herself in her room against a man who looked at her with that much *intent*. But she couldn't bring herself to do it. She couldn't let him see how much he affected her. She couldn't let him know how he got to her. *She couldn't.*

More than that, she couldn't seem to move.

He walked over to the little half wall and then, his eyes never leaving hers, he simply swung himself over it with an offhanded show of male grace that made everything inside Kathryn clench tight. Then run hot, pooling low in her belly and making her think she might simply melt where she stood. Making her think that perhaps she already had.

Luca didn't stop. He walked straight to her and he sank his hands in her hair and he hauled her close to him. To that mouth of his, dangerous and impossible and lush. To his flashing dark eyes that saw too much and condemned too deeply.

"What are you doing?" she asked again.

But her voice was a whisper, not a protest, and he knew it. She could tell by the way his fingers sank deeper into her hair, holding her that much more immobile.

"Sleepwalking, I think," he told her in that low voice of his that wound around inside her, making her burn. "It's a terrible habit. Worse than alcohol. There's no telling what I'll do in the middle of the night and then forget come morning."

"Luca—"

"I'll show you what I mean."

His voice was little more than a growl.

And then he slid his mouth over hers.

CHAPTER SIX

KATHRYN TOLD HERSELF it was a dream.

The moonlight. This man.

It was a dream, that was all, and so it didn't matter if she simply opened to him. If she let him sweep her up his bare chest, cool to the touch but still so hard, like steel. If she made no sign of protest.

If all she did was kiss him back as hungrily and greedily as if she'd been the one to go to him.

And everything was heat. Fire. Need and longing made real in the silvery night.

His hands were big and hard, slipping from her hair to cradle her face, holding her where he wanted her.

And he plundered her mouth, using his lips and his teeth and that clever tongue of his, angling his jaw to take the kiss deeper, wilder.

She felt dizzy again—unmoored and lost—and was only dimly aware that he'd hauled her off the ground and up into his arms. She didn't care. It was a dream, so what did it matter if he was carrying her somewhere, his mouth still fused to hers? He was tall and so very strong, and the feel of him surrounding her made her shake and quiver deep inside.

He walked back through her door and straight to her

bed, laying her across the piled-high linens and following her down into the clutch of all that softness, and it was…astonishing. There was no other word for the press of him against her, so male and darkly perfect, so hard and *Luca*. There was no other way to describe that absurdly sculpted body rubbing all over hers.

Making her feel new. Like a strange creature, red-hot and molten, taking over the body she'd thought until this moment she knew so well.

This is only a dream, she told herself, and so she indulged herself.

He stroked his way deep into her mouth, tasting her deeply, and she met him. She ran her fingers through that thick dark hair of his, crisp and warm to her touch. She traced the magnificent line of his wide, muscled back down to his narrow hips, then worked her way back up those *ridges* on his abdomen that she could admit, here in this dream where nothing counted, fascinated her to the point of distraction.

Beyond that point, perhaps.

He tore his mouth from hers even as his hands moved. He propped himself up on one forearm and smoothed his other hand over her cashmere top, pausing at the top and then tugging—and it was a measure of how dazed she was that she didn't comprehend what he was doing until he'd unzipped her and the cool air teased over her bare breasts.

And she was panting as if she was running. As if she'd been running for miles.

Luca muttered something in Italian that washed over her like a caress, and then he bent his head and took one nipple she hadn't realized had pebbled into a hard point deep into his mouth.

Kathryn heard a noise that could not possibly have been her, so high-pitched and keening, bouncing back from the canopy above them, the ornate ceiling. She felt the dark current of his laughter shake through him and into her, making his shoulders move beneath her hands and shudder against her breasts. The sheer physicality of that stunned her, and then he simply sucked on her, that rich tugging setting off an explosion inside her. It seared its way through her, like a lightning bolt from his mouth straight down the center of her body to kick between her legs.

Hard and something like beautiful, all at once.

And Kathryn didn't know what to do. There was too *much* of him, everywhere. All over her, pressing her down with him into the embrace of her soft, soft mattress, making her wish this mad dream could go on and on forever.

He made a low, greedy sound that she recognized somehow, in a deep feminine place inside her she'd never known was there, and thrilled to at once. She dug her hands in his hair, but not to guide him—only to anchor herself as he smoothed his wicked palm down over her exposed belly, pausing to test the indentation of her navel, then dipping even lower to slip beneath the waistband of her soft trousers.

Kathryn opened her mouth to speak, to say *something*— to *do* something—

But Luca knew exactly what he was about. He didn't pause. He simply slid his hand down, so hot and hard, and then held the core of her, molten and hot and swollen with need, in his palm.

She made a noise, and he laughed again. He used the faint edge of his teeth against her nipple and made that lightning bolt roar through her again, wider and hotter and far more dangerous, and then he ground the heel of his hand against the place she ached most.

And Kathryn disappeared. She went up in a column of flame that tore her apart. She lost herself, shattering into too many pieces to count. She shook and she shook, bucking against him and unable to stop or hold on or do anything but survive the explosion—and when she finally came back to earth it was with a giant thud and a heartbeat so hard against her ribs that it hurt.

It *hurt.*

There was no pretending *that* was a dream.

Luca's hand was still down her trousers, tracing lazy patterns in her wet heat, and he'd propped himself up next to her while he did it. Watching her. Learning her. And Kathryn found she couldn't quite breathe. Something he made that much worse when he shifted from watching his own hand play with her, letting his gaze slam into hers.

His eyes were dark. So very dark. There was something powerful and supremely knowing in the way he looked at her then, and she shuddered again, as if she couldn't keep herself from falling apart. As if now he needed only to look at her to make her crack wide-open.

"Luca…" But she didn't sound like herself. She didn't recognize that small, profoundly needy voice that came out of her own mouth.

And she had no idea what to say.

He murmured something else in Italian, a low string of syllables that danced over her the way he did as he moved down the bed, hooking his fingers in the waistband of her trousers and yanking them down over her hips. He peeled them down her legs and tossed them aside, and Kathryn was shaking. She couldn't stop shaking.

And she was still so hot. So needy. Helpless, somehow, in the face of all that yearning and that intense look on his beautiful face.

"Luca," she said again, forcing herself to speak because this wasn't a dream, and reality was coming at her as hard as if the canopy had collapsed above her, bringing the whole of the château down with it.

"I have to taste you," he growled at her, his voice thicker and rougher than she'd ever heard it before, and that, too, slicked through her like lightning. Then he said something in Italian, and that, somehow, was worse. Or better.

"I don't think…" she tried to say.

"Good. Don't think."

He moved to take her hips in his hands, then settled himself between her legs as if he belonged there. He wedged her thighs open with his sculpted shoulders, and then he made a growling sort of sound that made a wave of goose bumps crash over the whole of her body.

"Bellissima," he murmured, directly into the heart of her need.

And then he simply licked his way straight into her core.

She tasted sweet and hot, the richest cream and all woman, and Luca drank deep.

Kathryn went stiff beneath him, shuddering anew, her hands tugging at him as if she couldn't decide whether to pull him closer or shove him away.

He took her over. He licked and he hummed, throwing her straight back into that fire, until she was rolling her hips to get closer to his mouth, begging him with her body.

He was so hard he thought it might kill him.

He found his way to the hot little center of her and sucked, hard.

And Kathryn made a low sound, long and wild. Then she was bucking against him, her hoarse cry rebounding off the walls, shattering beneath him all over again, and if he had ever seen anything better in all his life, he couldn't recall it.

Luca waited her out. She sobbed something incomprehensible and he liked that. He liked it too much.

He knelt up, letting his gaze trace over her as she lay sprawled there before him, more beautiful than he could have imagined—and the truth was, he'd imagined this very thing far more often than he was comfortable admitting, even to himself.

Her breasts were the perfect small handfuls, tipped in rose, and the center of her femininity was slick and hot. The taste of her poured through him like fire, arousal and need, the spice of a woman and her own particular sweetness besides.

And even here, open and shuddering, splayed out before him, there was something about her. A certain innocence, however impossible that seemed, that made him that much harder—the need in him taking on a near vicious edge.

He shoved his hair back from his face and looked around, wondering where she kept her condoms. Because surely she had some. Or perhaps she dealt with birth control a different way entirely, which meant he could—

And Luca froze then.

Because if Kathryn was on birth control, that would have been to keep herself from getting pregnant *with his father.* To keep herself from giving birth to a child that would have been Luca's own sibling.

Disgust and self-loathing hit him like a blow. Like an attack. He felt dazed.

How could he have forgotten who she was? How could he have let this happen?

You didn't let *this happen, you fool*, he growled at himself. *You did this all yourself.*

Kathryn was a spider at best, and now he knew exactly how sweet her web was, and he was ruined. *Ruined.*

Damn her.

He pushed back, levering himself off the bed and letting the chill of the winter night, even here inside her bedroom, sink into him from his bare feet up. He hadn't been able to sleep. No surprise, given the direction of his thoughts and his knowledge that she'd slept *just there* on the other side of his wall.

He'd tortured himself with the temperature, bathing himself in the winter moon as if it had been a form of cold shower. He had no idea how long he'd been out there, fighting a pitched battle with an enemy that he knew wasn't Kathryn at all. It was him. It was this need in him, gripping him hard and mercilessly even now, making him want to forget all over again and lose himself in that sweet, dangerous oblivion between her thighs.

You are the worst kind of idiot, he told himself harshly.

He watched her come back to herself, flushed and satisfied and more beautiful than any woman should be.

And far more dangerously compelling than *this* woman should be, especially to him.

He hated himself.

He told himself he hated her more.

"Is this how you do it?" he asked, and his voice was as cold as the night outside. *"Stepmother?"*

Kathryn jerked against the pillows as if he'd thrown a bucket of cold water on her. She looked stunned for a moment, and Luca felt something snake through him, hot and low and much too black to bear. It felt a good deal like shame—but he refused to let that stop him.

His breath sawed out of his chest, and Kathryn didn't help things. She sat up slowly, as if she ached. As if she didn't understand what he'd done to her—what he was doing—and he hated that she could keep the act going even now. When he was still so hard it hurt, and worse, he knew how she tasted now. And she was rumpled and flushed from his hands and his mouth—yet looked at him with her gray eyes dark as if she couldn't comprehend how that had happened.

He gritted his teeth as she swallowed, so hard he heard it, and then tugged her clothing back into place. And his curse was that howling thing inside him that wanted to strip her down and worship her, glut himself in her, until this madness in him subsided. Until he could *think*.

"I'm touched by this performance," he told her, his voice a dark thing in the moonlit room. "Truly I am. You look nothing less than ravished and yet innocent besides, as if I didn't just make you come. Twice."

He watched the way she shivered. The way she pulled her longer sweater tighter around her as if it was made of chain mail and could fend him off. The way she didn't quite meet his gaze.

"As a matter of fact," she said, carefully, as if she wasn't sure of her own voice, "I'd prefer not to have this postmortem just now."

"I imagine you don't."

She swallowed again, and there was nothing but shadows in her eyes when she finally looked at him.

"You were sleepwalking," she said softly. "I was dreaming. This never happened."

"Yet it did," he gritted out at her. "I can still taste you."

She pulled her knees up beneath her and hugged them close, and he loathed himself. He did. She looked like a lost little girl, and he was still hard and furious, and beyond all of that, she was still his father's widow.

His father's widow.

"Why did you marry him?"

He didn't mean to ask that again. He didn't know why he had.

But this time, when she gazed back at him, her gray eyes were like storms.

"To torture you," she told him, her voice still hoarse, but something hard beneath it. "Is that what you want to hear?"

"I suspect that's not far from the truth, if likely not so personal."

She made a frustrated sort of noise and rolled off the bed—but kept her distance, he noticed, as she skirted around to its foot.

"I'm taking a bath," she said in a low tone. "I want to wipe this entire night off me." She looked at him over her shoulder. "Torture yourself all you want, Luca. But I'll thank you to do it somewhere else."

And this time when she walked away from him, Luca told himself he was glad of it. That it was better.

No matter that his body still wanted her.

But that was all the information he needed, surely. The things he wanted were always the things that destroyed him—his family being a case in point. That was why, so long ago now he could hardly remember anything else, he'd stopped allowing himself to want anything.

He would conquer this, too.

Kathryn decided to treat the entire situation as if it really had been a dream. Everyone had unfortunately detailed and potentially steamy dreams about coworkers sometimes, surely. The trick was acting as if it had only ever happened inside her head.

She told herself she could do that. Why not? Luca was the master at playing whatever role worked best for his purposes. She could do the same.

Though it was harder than she'd anticipated to walk into that breakfast room the way she'd done every other morning in California and act as if her body didn't flush into shivering awareness at the sight of him.

It was so unfair.

He was gorgeous and terrible, commanding his side of the table with that lazy authority of his that she felt as if his mouth against her center again, bold and insistent. He was dressed in one of his devastatingly perfect suits today, crisp and lethally masculine as if he hadn't been up half the night, and Kathryn forced herself to stand there with her usual serene smile on her face. She was determined to do her best to *look* as calm and un-ruffled as he did.

But there was no controlling that low, wild lick of pure fire that swept through her, curling itself into dark knots deep inside, then blooming into something greedy and consuming in her sex.

You are in so much trouble, a small voice whispered inside her.

Worse, she was sure he knew it. That he could *see* every last thing she tried to hide from him. When all she could see in him was that harsh light in his dark eyes and that dangerous look on his face.

"Don't loom there," he said, all silken threat and a kind of menace that made her pulse pick up. "Sit down. This is meant to be a breakfast meeting to outline my plans for the day, Kathryn." He waited for her to look at him. To meet that awful gaze of his that tore straight through her. "Not agony."

There was absolutely no reason that should make her feel as if she might swallow her tongue. Kathryn ordered herself to pull it together. She pulled out her graceful, high-backed chair and sat down, the same way she had every other morning on this endless trip that she worried would leave her a mere shell of herself before it was done.

Maybe it already had, she thought with a shiver she fought to repress when he did nothing more shocking than fill her cup with coffee, a rich, dark brew that she thought was the precise color of his furious eyes—

She needed to stop.

"Tonight will be a family event," Luca said in a con-trolled sort of way that made the fact of his temper a living thing, dancing there between them. All the more obvious because it was hidden. Controlled. Just as he always had been—except for last night. Kathryn had to conceal the shiver that moved through her then. "Rafael, Lily and I—and therefore you, as my personal shadow—are expected at another winery in Napa."

"The next valley over."

"Yes." He set the silver coffeepot down on the table between them with a hint of something like violence, if carefully restrained. "Your command of geography is impressive."

"As is your use of sarcasm."

"Careful, Kathryn." His voice seemed darker then. Deeper. Infinitely more dangerous. "I know too much about you now. Far too many secrets about what makes you…" He paused, and she flushed then. She couldn't help it, no matter that she saw that gleam of satisfaction in his dark gaze and hated the both of them. "Tick." He eyed her. "You should keep that in mind."

He meant sex. All of this was about sex, the last topic on earth she wanted to discuss—especially with him. But it shot through her anyway, flame and heat, like the word itself was a heavy stone plummeting from a great height. It hit bottom in that molten-hot place between her legs, where she could still feel him. Where no amount of soaking in that bath earlier had managed to wipe away the exquisite feel of his hands or his mouth. She felt branded. Marked.

Though she thought she'd rather die right where she sat than let him know it.

"I'm so glad you brought that up," she said crisply. "Obviously, what happened last night can never happen again. You are my late husband's son and my supervisor, not to mention the fact that you are anything but a fan of mine. I'm appalled that we got as carried away as we did."

"If you plan to clutch at your pearls, you should have worn some." Luca's voice sounded decadent then. Dark and rich, and with that lazy note to it besides, as if he was enjoying himself. "As it is, it's difficult to take anything you say seriously when I can see how hard your nipples are, Kathryn. I don't think the word you're looking for is *appalled*."

Kathryn would never know how she managed to keep herself from looking down at her own breasts then, where she could feel a traitorous tightening that suggested he was right. How she only stared back at him with a faintly pitying air instead.

"It's winter, Luca," she said, almost gently. "You're wearing a suit. I am not. Do you need me to explain how female biology works?"

And that impossibly golden smile of his flashed then, as beautiful and bright as it was totally unexpected.

"Do you?" he asked, and there was that same note in his voice that every part of her recognized, down into her bones. It took her a moment to place it.

I have to taste you, he'd growled at her last night before he'd done just that. In exactly this same way.

Kathryn went very still. Or he did. Or maybe it was the world that stopped for a long, taut moment, as if there was nothing but the pounding of her heart and that betraying *tightening* everywhere else. As if he really could see straight into her. As if he knew. As if, were she to give him the slightest signal, he'd simply sweep all the breakfast things off the table and haul her across it, setting his mouth to her the way he had in all that silvery moonlight.

How could she fear him and want him at the same time?

"Good morning."

Rafael's voice from the doorway cut through the tension between them as if he'd used one of the ceremonial swords that hung theatrically in the château's tasting room in another part of the winery.

Kathryn told herself it was a relief. That it was *relief* that coursed through her, syrupy and thick.

She swiveled to face him, entirely too aware that Luca did the same thing—entirely too aware of Luca, come to that.

Rafael's cool gaze moved between them. From Luca to Kathryn and then back, and Kathryn was suddenly certain that he knew. That he could *see* what had happened between them, that he could hear the echo of those impossible cries she'd made into the night, that she was marked bright red and obvious.

"Lily and I won't be coming with you tonight" was all he said, in that remote way of his that made him such an excellent CEO. "She's having some contractions, and it's better that she stay off her feet."

"Is she all right?" Kathryn asked, frowning. "Isn't it a little bit early?" And then she regretted it when two pairs of dark and speculative Castelli eyes fixed on her in a way she didn't like at all. She forced a smile. "I beg your pardon. Am I not allowed to ask now that I'm merely a Castelli Wine employee?"

"No," Luca said at once. "It makes me question your motives."

"You would do that anyway," she replied smoothly,

without looking at him. "As far as I can tell, it's your favorite pastime."

Rafael smiled, and Kathryn was certain she didn't like the way he did it. "Lily is fine, Kathryn. Thank you for asking. This is nothing particularly worrisome, but her doctor would prefer she put her feet up for a few days, and that means another work event would be too much."

He aimed that smile at his brother then, and it took on a sharper edge that even Kathryn could feel. She was aware of Luca stiffening at his place across the table.

And of Rafael, still there in the doorway, his gaze entirely too assessing. "But it looks as if you have things as well in hand as ever, brother. I leave it to you."

CHAPTER SEVEN

HALFWAY THROUGH THE formal dinner laid out with luxurious attention to detail in one of the Napa winery's private rooms up high on a hillside, every plate and glass and carefully arranged bit of food as choreographed as some refined ballet, Luca was so darkly furious he had no idea how he kept to his seat.

He told himself it wasn't fury. Or it shouldn't have been. That Kathryn was simply doing what she did, what she had always done and always would, and there was no point reacting to it at all—

But that didn't help. Every time her musical little laugh floated across the table, he tensed. Every time that silver-haired jackass to her left with the wandering hands touched her, he thought smoke might pour from his ears.

It was one thing to know that this was what she did. That she was no doubt lining up potential selections for her future wherever she went. He'd never expected anything less. Yet it turned out it was something else to witness her in action.

Particularly when he could still *feel* her. Still hear those cries in his ears. Still taste her, the hard nub of her nipple and that creamy heat below.

Damn her.

He had no memory of the conversations he must have engaged in with the people sitting on either side of him. When the eternal dinner ground to an end at last and he could finally get the hell away, he escorted Kathryn to their waiting car with a hand that was, he could admit, perhaps a little too insistent against the small of her back.

"Is this an attempt at chivalry or are you herding me?" she asked under her breath, that damned smile of hers still welded into place even outside, in the dark, where there was no one to see her but him.

He wanted to mess her up, Luca acknowledged. He wanted to dig his fingers beneath that facade of hers and see what she hid away underneath. He wanted far too much, and all of it wrong. And dangerous, besides.

He was not a man who had ever been interested in entanglements. But *tangled* was the very least of the things he felt around this woman.

Luca held the passenger door of the sleek limousine open as she climbed inside, nodding brusquely at their driver. Then he swung into the limo's hushed interior himself, making no particular attempt to keep to his own side of the wide backseat as he slammed the door shut behind him.

Kathryn was digging in her evening bag. She glanced at him as he came close, then froze.

"What's the matter?" she asked. The faintest frown etched itself between her eyes, where that fringe of hers nearly touched her eyes and drove him utterly crazy with that same sharp longing he was finding it harder and harder—impossible—to control. Just as he could no longer seem to control himself. "What happened?"

"You tell me."

He felt outsized and more than a little maddened. He sprawled there next to her, too close but not quite touching her. Not quite. His blood was pumping through him much too fast. His heart was trying to kick its way out of his chest. He was holding himself back by the smallest thread.

He wasn't sure how he was holding himself back at all.

Her frown deepened, which was at least better than that damned smile.

"I don't know, Luca. I thought that went well enough. I'm not sure what you wanted out of it, but it seems as if every vintner in two valleys is deeply impressed with your varietals. What more can you ask?"

For the first time in his life, Luca did not care the slightest bit about wine or the wine business or anything having to do with his damned vines or vintages or barrels or whatever else.

"I could ask that when we are conducting business, you manage to keep your mind on that," he seethed at her. He didn't even try to contain that tone of his or the simmering outrage in it. "And not on laying your trap for your next victim."

Her gray eyes chilled. "What are you talking about?"

"You weren't particularly subtle," he gritted at her as the car began to move, sweeping them out toward the main road and the mountains to the west. "Everyone at the table got to watch you hang all over that poor man and play your little games with him."

"And by *little games*, I assume you mean the work you and I were there to do? That I was doing while you sulked?"

"You spent a long time off in the bathroom before dessert," he continued, not caring that he could see the effect of his harsh tone in the way she shivered slightly. "What were you doing, I wonder? Your target also disappeared for a similar span of time. And God only knows what you were doing beneath the table where no one could see."

He'd thought of little else. He knew the meal he'd been served had been the finest Californian cuisine, a fusion of the state's rich bounty presented to perfection, and yet it had all been tasteless and pointless to him.

Kathryn shook her head, her lips pressing together. "This is ridiculous. Not to mention offensive in the extreme." Her gray eyes flashed. "Of course, that's your thing, isn't it? The more horrible, the better."

"And here's what I wonder." He shifted so he was closer to her, looming over her, his whole body humming with that darkness, that tension, that driving need he could neither understand nor control. This was what she did to him. She made him lose the tight control he'd always maintained over himself, his world, his life. Always. He found that the most unforgivable. Maybe that was what made him move his face that much closer to hers—so she could *feel* his fury in every word he spoke. "How does a noted whore for hire seal the deal? On your knees or on your back? Does it vary with each mark or do you stick to a set routine?"

He didn't see her move, and that told him more about the blind single-mindedness of that darkness in him than anything else. He felt her palm against his jaw, heard the *crack* of it fill the car's interior with the bright burst of the slap she delivered and he saw the fire and the fury in her dark gray eyes.

The pain came a moment later, sharp and swift.

"You're a vile little man," she threw at him, and he didn't disagree with her. But that was neither here nor there. "The only thing more disgusting than your imagination is the fact you think you can dump it out on me whenever you feel like it, like a toxic spill."

Luca laughed, a darker sound than the night outside the car or the way her breath came out in angry pants, and tested his jaw with his hand.

"That actually hurt." He shifted his gaze to hers, and eyed the way she sat there, clearly trembling with rage. "Is this where you play the outraged and offended virgin? I must tell you, Kathryn. You're not that accomplished an actress."

She paled. He thought she might keel over, or explode, but she pressed her lips together again instead. She lifted a hand, and he thought she might try to hit him once more—and the operative word was *try*—but she only put her palm to her neck. As if she wanted to control her own pulse. Or her own breath.

Or herself.

And he didn't know what to do with that notion that swept over him like heat, that she might find herself as out of control in the middle of this mess as he clearly was.

"If you hit me again," he told her softly, "I'll return the favor."

"You'll hit me?" Her eyes were grim in the dark. "I'm glad your father is dead, Luca. He would have been horrified by you."

He ignored the little flare of something a good deal like shame deep inside him then, even as it knotted itself in his gut.

"Let's be very clear about this," he said, and he was aware on a distant level that the fury that had been riding him all through dinner had eased. Not disappeared, but loosened its hold. He didn't ask himself why. "It will be a very cold day in hell before I worry myself over what my father, of all people, might have thought about anything I do. Much less what you think. That's the moral equivalent of taking lectures on good behavior from the devil himself." He eyed her in the close confines of the car's backseat, where he was still too much in her space, and it still wasn't enough. Not close enough. Not *enough*. "But I don't hit women. Not even when they've hit me first."

She had the grace to look faintly abashed at that, and her gaze dropped to her hand. She flexed her fingers out in front of her, and he wondered if her palm stung as much as his jaw did. The idea didn't make that heavy knot inside him loosen any.

He reached over and took her hand in his, and held on when she tried to jerk it out of his grasp. He ignored the little *huff* of air that escaped her lips, and smoothed his fingers over her palm as if he was tracing it. As if he wanted to rub the sting out.

As if he didn't know what the hell he wanted.

"Hit me again, Kathryn," he said in a low voice, looking at her hand instead of her face, "and I'll take that as an invitation to finish what we started last night. No matter how many old men you make dance to your tune at a dinner table. No matter who you're pretending to be tonight."

Her fingers curled as if she wanted to clench them into a fist.

"I'm not pretending to be anyone," she snapped at

him. "The only person playing a game here is you. And there will never be an invitation to finish anything. That was an aberration. A terrible, horrifying mistake. I have no idea why it happened and—"

"Don't you?"

He hadn't meant to ask that question, but once out, it seemed to hover there between them, threatening everything. Pounding in him so hard it became indistinguishable from his own heartbeat.

"No," she whispered, but her gray eyes were too large and too dark. Her pretty mouth trembled with the lie of it. And he could feel the tremor she fought to repress in that hand he held between his. "I have no idea what you're talking about. I never do."

And Luca smiled. Hard. "Let me give you some clarity."

He let go of her hand and reached for her, wrapping his hands around her waist and lifting her out of her seat and over his lap. He heard her breath desert her as he settled her against him, her legs to one side. Then he simply bent his head and took her mouth with his.

Once again, that maddening fire. Once again, that swift shock, lust and need, greed and hunger, burning him alive.

As hot and as wild as if they were still in her bed. As if they'd never left, never stopped.

And she didn't fight him. She didn't pretend. He felt her give in to this thing that pounded between them, felt the heady rush of her surrender.

She hooked her arms around his neck as if she couldn't control herself any more than he could, then she opened her mouth to him and kissed him back.

And Luca lost track of everything.

That he was trying to make a point. That they were in the back of a moving car. That she was the last woman on earth he should be touching at all, much less like this. That he absolutely should not be doing this.

He simply lost himself in the perfection of her mouth. The sweet heat of the way she kissed him and tangled her fingers in his hair. The weight of her slender body against his and the sheer desperation in the way they came together.

Again and again.

But it wasn't enough.

He groaned against her mouth, and she shifted against him as if he'd lit her on fire, the curve of her hip coming up hard against his aching sex.

And Luca stopped pretending he had any control where this woman was concerned. Or at all.

He shifted her on top of him, swinging her around to straddle him. He shoved the dress she wore up and out of his way, settling her down astride his lap, and he almost lost it when she gasped into his mouth as the softest part of her came up flush against his hardness.

He could feel her shudder all around him, or maybe that was him, as lost in this insanity as she was.

There was no control. There was no hint of it. And the truly scary part of that was how little Luca cared that it was gone.

There was nothing but his hands buried in her hair again and his mouth against hers, feasting on her. Ravishing her. He could feel her wet heat against him and rolled himself into it, aware that only the fabric of his trousers and the insubstantial panties she wore separated them. He let the slick, hot glory of it build.

There was nothing but her taste, an addictive wildness against his tongue. She surrounded him, more beautiful with her dress at her waist and her hair half–falling down from its elegant little knot than any other woman he'd ever seen.

Than anything at all.

And Luca found himself muttering things he knew better than to say out loud, even if he was speaking in Italian.

"Tu sei mia," he told her. *You are mine.* He didn't know where that had come from, what the hell he was doing. Why he meant such things down deep in his bones, when he shouldn't. When he couldn't.

But he found he didn't much care then. He filled his hands with the taut curves of her bottom and guided her against him in an unapologetically carnal rhythm, until she tilted her head back and moaned.

So he did it even harder, watching her face go slack as she rocked against him, driving him crazy, making him so hard and ready for her it bordered on pain. He moved his hand from her gorgeous bottom, sliding it around to find the heat of her with his fingers through the barrier of those soft panties.

"Look at me, Kathryn," he ordered her, his voice little more than a growl.

She obeyed. And her eyes were wide and gray. Slicked hot with desire. Her lips were parted, and her cheeks were flushed. Luca felt something shift inside him, a sharp and uncompromising tilt. He couldn't name it, though there was no pretending he didn't feel it. He only knew that he was no longer the same man he'd been even five minutes before.

There was only Kathryn, arched above him, straining against him, her beautiful eyes locked on to his.

And there is this, he thought, sliding his hands into her panties and slicking his way through the molten wildfire of her sweet core to find the neediest part of her. Then he pressed down, hard and sure, and watched her hurtle over the side of the world.

She bucked against him as her pleasure tumbled through her, making greedy little noises that were almost his undoing, her fingers digging hard into his shoulders, her head thrown back and her lovely back arched like a bow.

And everything shifted again, but this time, all the hunger and greed and sense in his body surged straight to his sex.

Luca needed to be inside her. Right now.

She was still shaking, still astride him. She was still panting as she tipped forward until she could rest her forehead against his shoulder. And now he could feel her harsh little breaths as well as hear them, and somehow, that made everything hotter.

Closer. Crazier. Better.

He reached between them, amazed to find his hand was unsteady as he pulled himself from his trousers at last, so aching and so hard. Kathryn was limp now, still shuddering and gasping, and he simply pulled her panties to one side and lined himself up with her entrance, the scalding heat of her nearly enough to make him lose it right there.

He thought he swore in Italian, or perhaps it was a prayer. She was slick and hot, and he didn't care where else she'd been or with whom. He didn't care why. He didn't care about anything but the way she fit in his arms, his lap.

He didn't care about anything but this.

It had been two years of sheer torment with this woman; he could admit that now, when the truth seemed so obvious at last. He'd wanted her from the moment he'd first laid eyes on her. Perhaps he would always want her. But that wasn't something Luca wanted to think about. Not now when she was everything he'd ever wanted, poised there above him, hot and wet and nearly his.

Nearly.

He moved his hands to her hips to hold her right where he wanted her. He tucked his mouth against her neck, where he could taste her, salt and need.

And then finally, finally, he thrust his way home.

It hurt.

God, did it hurt.

Kathryn felt something tear, felt a shriek of agony sear through her like a burn, and then there was nothing but the hugeness of him. Deep, deep inside her. So deep she found she couldn't breathe, couldn't think, couldn't do anything but freeze there over him, that harsh thrust of his possession like a throbbing brand within her.

Luca swore.

Then again, in both Italian and English, and she scrunched up her face so she wouldn't cry and kept it buried in the crook of his shoulder as if she could hide from this. As if that might make the shuddering, aching heaviness go away.

But it didn't work.

"Look at me," he said, his voice hoarse. "Kathryn. Sit up."

"I don't want to."

He was still buried deep inside her, though he didn't

move. Then the car bumped over a dip in the road and thrust him deeper into her, and she felt the way he braced himself. Heard the small exhalation he made, as if this was no easier for him than it was for her. And that heavy sharpness radiated out from where the length of him was still inside her, making even her breasts feel stung with it.

As if the whole of her body was one giant *ache*.

"Sit up, *cucciola mia*," he said, in a voice she'd never heard him use before, something far warmer and indulgent than any she associated with him. He nudged her with his jaw. "Now, please."

And it seemed the hardest thing she'd ever done, to ease herself back, knowing he could see the panic and the pain and the leftover heat all over her face. To *feel him* lodged *inside* her as she carefully shifted position. To look into his dark eyes, so close to hers, aware that he knew things about her now she hadn't wanted to share.

Too many things.

It had all happened too fast. She'd been lost in another bone-deep, impossible shattering, torn apart into a million little pieces and unable to breathe, and then it had been too late.

Too late, she thought again.

She wasn't sure what that thing was that crept over her, deep in her chest and her gut, a raw sort of hollow. She was terribly afraid it might be a sob.

Luca reached up and smoothed her hair back from her still-flushed face. She squirmed against that thick, hard intrusion that connected them so intimately, and he only watched her do it. He didn't move—though she thought that steel line of his jaw hardened.

"Why didn't you tell me?" he asked, his voice the

quietest she'd ever heard it, and she didn't know what to make of that. She didn't know how to feel.

She moved her hips and didn't understand how people did this, or *why*, when there was no comfortable position and too much of that heavy, aching heat. "I didn't think you'd notice."

"Kathryn," he said, that low voice at odds, somehow, with the very nearly tender way his thumbs brushed over her temples, and her name in his mouth a kind of poetry that made that hollow thing inside her seem to hum. "You went from pleasure to pain in an instant. How could I not notice that?"

She shifted again, still trying to find a way to sit on his lap when he was *inside her*, and this time his eyes darkened. She caught her breath.

The car bumped again and this time, the sensations that spun out from that involuntary thrust were more of a deep spark than anything sharp or painful. The ache inside her...changed. The spark seemed to light it up, infusing it with something else besides the pain. She shifted experimentally, then tugged her bottom lip between her teeth when that *something else* bloomed into something better, and watched that slow hunger burn in his dark eyes.

She felt an answering echo of it in her, as if the heaviness and the stretched ache were connected to all that delicious heat she thought of as his, that she could feel easing back into her the longer they sat like this.

"I wasn't aware that it would matter to you whether or not you hurt me," she said, without meaning to speak.

Luca's hands moved to cup her cheeks, and his dark

eyes met hers, nearly grim in the shadows of this car slipping through the California night.

"It matters," he said gruffly. "You should have told me."

And that hollow thing inside her swelled, crashing over her like a terrible tide. She didn't know what it was. She only felt the sting of tears in her eyes and the throb of something far heavier in her chest.

And Luca deep inside her, hot and still.

"Tell you?" she whispered, because her voice had deserted her. "How could I tell you? You don't just think I'm a whore, Luca. You *know* it. You've never had the slightest doubt."

"Kathryn."

"You wouldn't have believed me." She only realized that her tears had spilled out when he wiped them away with his thumbs, more gentle with her than made any sense. "You would have laughed in my face."

He didn't deny that, though his gaze darkened even further.

He pulled her face to his and kissed her, and it was almost too much. The thrust of him deep inside her body and the impossible sweetness of his lips on hers. It made her brain short out. It made that great rawness inside her glow.

"Ah, *cucciola mia*," he murmured, pulling back from her mouth, still holding her face in his hands—almost as if he found her somehow precious. "I'm not laughing now."

And then he began to move.

CHAPTER EIGHT

KATHRYN TENSED, BUT Luca only pulled out slowly and then pressed back in, far more gently this time.

It didn't hurt. It felt...strange, but that was better than the pain.

"Breathe," he told her, in that bossy way of his that shouldn't have made something ignite inside her. But she did it anyway.

She pulled in a deep breath and let it out, and still he moved inside her. Lazy. Relaxed. An easy sort of rocking.

Slowly, almost despite herself, Kathryn began to anticipate him. She met him when he thrust in, moving her hips in a way that made a low, shimmering thing dance inside her.

His mouth curved, and she thought that later—much later—she would have to examine why it was that it made her flush with so much pleasure.

He maintained that same lazy pace, and let his hands wander where they pleased. He smoothed his way up her back. He tested the thrust of her breasts through the dress that was still bunched around her waist. He reached beneath it and drew patterns on the soft skin of her belly, on the outsides of her thighs.

Kathryn found herself moving more, rolling her hips and testing the depth of his stroke. *This* dragged the center of her against him, and it made everything inside her wind up tight. *That* made a sweet shudder work its way up her spine. She tried different movements, wriggling against him and rocking into him, and he let her, only that heavy-lidded heat in his dark eyes and the faint flush high on his cheekbones a hint that he felt the same fire she did.

And slowly, surely, inevitably, she forgot that anything had ever hurt her. There was nothing but the glide, the pull. The bright heat that expanded the deeper he went into her and the more she met each thrust.

There was a coiling thing inside her, huge and terrifying, and Kathryn didn't know which she wanted more—to hide from it or throw herself straight into its center. And in any case, it didn't matter. Because Luca let out a delicious little laugh as if he knew exactly what she felt, and took control.

He pulled her hips flush with his. He took her mouth in a deep, dark, endless kiss. And he began to move within her in earnest, each slick thrust making that coil wind tighter, making it bigger and wilder and that much more intense.

And she couldn't. She couldn't—

"You can," he said against her mouth, and she realized she'd said that out loud. "You will."

And he shifted beneath her, then ran his clever fingers down to the place they were joined, and rubbed.

The next time he thrust inside her, she imploded. A brilliant, impossible shattering that rolled out from the place where he maintained that demanding pace, tearing her soul from her body and her limbs apart.

She heard him groan out her name, his mouth against her neck, and then he toppled right over that same cliff beside her.

And for a very long time, that was all there was.

When Kathryn came back to herself, she was still slumped against him and still astride him, and the car was slowing to make its final turn into the Castelli vineyard.

She pushed herself back up to a sitting position and climbed off Luca at the same time, feeling the loss of that length of him inside her like a blow. It made her feel even more awkward as she struggled to wriggle her dress back into place. Even more…off center.

He didn't speak. She didn't dare look at him. She heard him zip himself up, and then there was the long drive up from the road to the château to endure in the same heavy silence. Kathryn felt too many things, thought too many things, all of them battering at her like a thousand desperate winds, but she couldn't let herself do that here. Not while he was still beside her, so male and so hard, and now something entirely different than what he'd been even an hour before.

She didn't want to change. She didn't want the shift. She didn't understand how she'd simply…surrendered to him when she was twenty-five years old and hadn't felt the slightest urge to give herself to anyone in all her years.

"You're much too pretty," her mother had told her when she was barely thirteen, with a frown that told Kathryn that this was not a positive thing. "Mind you don't let it make you lazy. *Pretty* is nothing more than a prison sentence. Best you remember that before you let it turn your head."

And she'd tried. She'd buried herself in her studies. She'd run from the slightest hint of male interest or even friendships with girls who had any kind of active social lives, lest she be tempted into joining in. She'd done everything she could think of to prove to her mother that her looks weren't a weakness, that she could take advantage of the gifts Rose had given her with all her scrimping and saving and hard work.

But Rose had never been convinced.

"They'll trap you if they can," she'd told Kathryn again and again throughout her teenage years. "Tell you it's love. There's no such thing, my girl. There are only men who will leave you and babies who need raising once they're gone. A pretty thing like you will be easy pickings."

And Kathryn had resolved that whatever else she was, she wouldn't be *that.*

Even at university she'd been good at holding herself apart, keeping herself safe. She didn't want boyfriends or even supposed male friends who might think they could get to her that way, when her defenses were down. She avoided any scenario that might lead to lowered inhibitions or the slightest hint of danger. No pubs with her classmates. No parties. She'd kept herself in her own little tower, locked safely away, where nothing and no one could ever touch her or ruin her or make her a disappointment to her mother, who had given up so much to make her life possible.

All this time, she thought now, as the limo pulled up to the château's grand entrance, and Rose had been right. It really was a slippery slope, and Kathryn had plummeted straight down it and crashed at the bottom. One single car ride with a man who despised her, and she'd lost a lifetime of her moral high ground, her entire self-definition. She'd become exactly what Luca had always accused her of being, what Rose had always darkly intimated she'd become one day whether she liked it or not.

The whole world was different. *She* was different. And she didn't have the slightest idea how to come to terms with any of it, or what it meant.

The driver opened the door, and Kathryn climbed out too quickly, shocked when she felt twinges in all sorts of unfamiliar places. She might have toppled to the ground, but Luca was there, taking her arm as if he'd anticipated this. Holding her steady.

Though he still didn't say a word.

Kathryn pulled her arm out of his grasp, aware that he let her do it, and felt a rush of sheer, hot embarrassment wash over her. She couldn't read that expression on his face, making him look like granite in the light that beamed out from the château's windows and the moon high above. She couldn't imagine what she must look like—wrinkled and rumpled, used and altered, like a walking neon advertisement for what she'd just done. Was it written on her face? Would the whole world be able to *see* what had happened right there—what she'd done? What she'd let him do?

The notion made her panic.

She all but ran up the steps and threw open the door, relieved that there was no sign of anyone around as she hurtled herself inside the château's ornate entry hall like a missile.

It's fine, she told herself, though she didn't believe it. Though she could hear the drumming panic in her own head. *Everything is perfectly fine.*

She made herself slow down. She was aware of Luca just behind her, a solid wall of regret at her heels, but she told herself to ignore it. To pretend he wasn't there. She forced herself to walk, not run. She headed up the stairs and then down the hall that led to the family wing. She made her way all the way to the far end of the château, and then finally, *finally*, she could see the door to her own room. She couldn't wait to close herself inside and…breathe.

She would take another very long bath. She would scrub all of this away. She would curl herself up into a tiny little ball, and she would not permit herself to cry.

She would not.

Luca said her name when she'd finally reached her door, when she had her hand out to grab the handle and was *this close—*

And Kathryn didn't want this. She didn't want whatever cutting, eviscerating, gut punch of a thing he was about to say. Whatever new and inventive way he'd come up with to call her a whore and make her feel like one.

But she wanted him to know how fragile she was even less, so she turned around and faced him.

He stood much too close, his dark eyes glittering, an expression she couldn't place on his beautiful face. She wished he wasn't so gorgeous, that he didn't make her ache. She imagined that might make it easier— might make that tugging thing near her heart dissipate more quickly.

She should say something; she knew she should. But she couldn't seem to make her mouth work.

"Where are you going, *cucciola mia*?" he asked softly.

She hated him, she told herself. The only thing worse

than his insults was this. That softness she couldn't understand at all.

"I don't know what that means. I don't speak any Italian."

His mouth moved into that curve again, and his dark eyes were much too intense. He reached over and tucked a strand of her hair behind her ear, and Kathryn knew he could feel the way that made her shudder. And her breath catch.

"I suppose it means *my pet*, more or less," Luca said, as if he hadn't considered it until that moment.

And the true betrayal was the warmth that spread through her at that, as if it was that laugh of his, bottled up, pure liquid sunshine starting deep inside her. Because he was dangerous enough when he was hateful. Kathryn thought that this other side of him—what she might have called *affectionate* had they been other people—might actually kill her.

Her throat felt swollen. Scratchy. Because of the noises she'd made in that car that she couldn't let herself think about? Or because of that brand-new rawness lodged inside her now? She didn't know. But she forced herself to speak anyway. "I don't want to be your pet."

That curve of his mouth deepened. "I don't know that it's up to you."

Kathryn felt restless. Edgy. As if she might burst. Or scream. Or simply crumple to the ground—and he seemed perfectly content to stand there forever, seeing things in her face she was quite certain she'd prefer to hide.

She scowled at him. "I don't know what you want from me."

This time, when he reached out, he took her shoulders in his hands and tugged her into his arms, and when he wrapped his arms around her, she melted. God help her, but she simply...fell into him. All that heat and strength, enveloping her like some kind of benediction.

"Come," he said quietly, letting her go. "I'll show you."

Kathryn knew what she needed to do. What her mother would expect her to do. One slip was bad enough. One terrible mistake. There was still time to save herself. There was still the possibility that she could call tonight a lost battle and go on to win the war, surely. She needed only to pull away from him, step inside her room and lock him out, so she could set about the Herculean task of putting herself back together.

But she couldn't make herself do it.

And when Luca opened the door to his bedroom and held out his hand as if he knew exactly what battles she was fighting and, more than that, how to win them, Kathryn ignored the great riot and tumult that shook inside her, and took it.

Luca didn't know how to make sense of any of this.

And that lost look in her too-dark gray eyes, something too close to broken, was too much for him. He had a thousand questions he didn't ask. A thousand more stacked behind them. He had the sense that there was something lying in wait for him, just over his shoulder or perhaps deep inside him, that he didn't care to examine.

Not tonight, when he'd discovered that she was precisely as innocent as she'd sometimes appeared.

It didn't matter how or why. Even the subject of her marriage to his father could wait.

What mattered—what beat in him like a darkening pulse that only got louder and more insistent with every breath—was that whatever else happened, whatever games she played or was playing even now, whatever the hell was going on here in all this California moonlight, she was his.

His.

Luca didn't wish to question himself on that. On why that surge of sheer possession seared through him, as if she'd branded him somehow with the unexpected gift of her innocence. He only knew that she was his. Only his.

And Luca wasn't done with her. Not even close.

She put her hand in his and let him lead her into his rooms, and there was no particular reason that should feel like trumpets blaring, drums pounding, a whole damned parade. But it did.

It should horrify him, he knew, that he had so little control where this woman was concerned—but tonight he couldn't bring himself to care.

He took his time.

He stood her at the foot of the great platform bed and undressed her slowly, not letting her help. He slid her shoes from her feet. He found the hidden side zipper on the bodice of her dress and eased it down, then tugged the whole of it up and over her head. He unhooked the bra she wore and pulled it from her arms, letting it fall to the floor with the rest.

When she stood before him in nothing but those panties he'd shoved out of his way in the car and that uncertain look on her face that he thought might kill him, Luca took a moment to ease his fingers through her hair. He pulled out what remained of that upswept knot she'd worn to dinner. He stroked his hands through the thick, straight strands, comforting them both.

And only when she let out a long breath he didn't think she knew she'd been holding did he finish undressing her, easing her panties down over her hips and then over the length of her perfectly formed legs.

Luca let himself look at her for a long time, indulging that possessive streak he'd never known he had. Because he'd never felt anything like it before tonight. He shrugged out of his jacket and kicked off his shoes. Still he gazed at her, letting her exquisite beauty imprint itself deep inside him. Every part of her was lovely, so astonishingly perfect that something moved in him at the sight, equal parts need and alarm.

He swept her up into his arms, enjoying the tiny noise she made, and then he carried her into the bathroom suite. He set her down next to the tub and ran the water, tossing in a handful of bath salts as it began to fill.

"Are we taking a bath?" Her voice cracked and she flushed, and Luca understood that this was a Kathryn he'd never seen before, this unsteady, uncertain creature who suddenly seemed much younger and far more breakable to him.

Or this has always been Kathryn, a voice in him suggested, more sharply than was strictly comfortable. *And you have been nothing but an ass.*

He shoved that aside, ruthlessly. There would be time enough to address the great mess of things that waited for him with the dawn.

Tonight was about this. Tonight was about her.

Instead of answering her, he stripped, watching her color rise the more he revealed. He was fascinated. Mesmerized by that spread of color, from her cheeks down her neck, to turn even her chest a pale pink, a shade or two lighter than the rose of her upturned nipples.

He wanted to feast on her. All of her.

When they were both naked he urged her into the hot water, settling her in front of him and between his legs with her back to him. He took the heavy mass of her thick dark hair in his hands and carefully made a new knot of it, high on the top of her head, and then wrapped his arms around her and held her there against him.

He didn't let himself think about anything. Just the sheer perfection of her body against his. The silken slide of the salted water, making her skin a smooth caress against his. He waited as she relaxed in increments against him, as she softened and, eventually, sighed. And only then did he begin to wash her.

He took his time. He touched her everywhere. He put his hands on every inch of her skin, saving that slippery heat between her legs for last, and a hard sort of satisfaction gripped him when she let out a hungry little moan at his touch.

Only when he'd made sure she was utterly boneless did he finish, standing her up and toweling her off, then carrying her back into the bedroom to put her in his bed at last. Her gaze never left him, wide and nearly green, and he'd learned her tonight. He knew what that faint quiver in her body meant. How she flushed when he crawled over her, a bright red on top of the pink she'd turned in the heat of the bath.

And when he was fully stretched out above her, skin to skin, he learned her all over again.

With his hands, his mouth. His tongue and his teeth.

He explored her. She'd given him something he could

hardly get his head around, could barely understand, and this was how he expressed his gratitude. His wonder. All those tangled things inside him that he knew better than to look at too closely. He worked them out against her lovely body, inch by perfect inch.

She arched up beneath him and he feasted on her breasts. She rocked against him and he held her down, tracing every muscle and every smooth curve, making her his. Making every last part of her inarguably his.

And this time, when he surged inside her, she was soft and shaking and ready for him.

She cried out his name.

Luca set a more demanding pace, gathering her beneath him, lost in the sleek glory of her hips against his. He built her up high. He made her sob. And then he threw her straight off that cliff and into bliss.

Once, then again.

And only then, when she was shattered twice over, her eyes slate green and filled with him and nothing else, did he follow her over that edge.

CHAPTER NINE

It was not until the following morning—after Luca had woken up to discover that none of the previous night had been one of the remarkably detailed dreams he'd had about Kathryn over the past couple of years, because she was still there, sprawled out beside him and wholly irresistible—that he allowed himself to think about what the inescapable fact of her innocence meant.

First, he'd rolled over, instantly awake and aware and as hard for her as if he'd never had her. She'd come awake a moment later, and he'd watched her eyes go from sleepy to pleased to wary in the course of a few blinks.

He'd found he hadn't cared much for *wary.*

So he'd pinned her hands above her head and settled himself between her thighs. He'd expressed his feelings on her tender breasts until she'd been gasping and arching beneath him, and then he'd driven himself home once again, losing himself in all her molten sweetness.

And he'd found the sound of her gasping his name as she convulsed around him far, far preferable to any wariness.

He managed to control himself in the shower they shared—but barely—and maybe the fact that doing so was so much harder than it should have been kicked his brain back into gear.

Kathryn was dressing, her head bent and a certain set expression on her face that he didn't like. He stood in the doorway to the bathroom with only a towel wrapped around his hips and watched her, aware that he should not be feeling any of the things that stampeded through him then. He knew that expression she wore. He usually liked it when the women he bedded showed him that particular blankness, because it meant they planned to walk away from him with no fuss. And quickly.

He didn't want her to walk away.

He wanted her right here, and he didn't care how crazy that was. How insane this entire situation was. That no one but him—that no one, *especially* him—would ever believe that *Saint Kate* had been a virgin until now.

"Kathryn." She didn't precisely jolt when she heard her name, but that wariness was back in her gaze when she lifted it to his. "Why did you marry him?"

She pressed her lips together in that way of hers that he should not find so fascinating. She tugged her bra into place and then bent to pick up her crumpled dress, frowning at it in a way that made something in the vicinity of his heart clench. Luca didn't speak. He swept up his own discarded shirt and prowled over to her, watching the way her eyes widened as he approached. Her lips parted slightly, as if she needed more air, and he couldn't pretend he didn't like that.

He liked entirely too much. Her lush little body, packaged in that lacy bra and matching panties that highlighted parts of her he could never obsess about *enough*. The faint marks from his mouth, his unshaven jaw. He was a primitive creature, he understood then, though he'd never thought of himself in those terms before. When it came to Kathryn, he was nothing short of a beast.

Luca liked his mark on her. He liked it hard and deep, so much it very nearly hurt.

He settled his dress shirt around her shoulders, then tugged her arms through. And then he took his time buttoning it up, fashioning her a dress that was much too big for her frame, but was in its way another mark. Another brand.

The beast within him roared its approval.

"Are you going to answer me?" he asked in a low voice as he rolled up one cuff, then the other, to keep the sleeves from hanging nearly to her knees.

She swallowed, and he saw that her eyes had changed color again, to that slate green that meant she was aroused. *Good*, he thought. He didn't imagine he'd ever be anything but aroused in her presence again. He wasn't sure he ever had been anything else, come to that.

But she blinked it away and took in a shuddering sort of breath.

"He said he could help," she said.

She moved away from him, and the sight of her in his shirt did things to Luca that he couldn't explain. He didn't want to explain them. They simply settled inside him, like light.

"Why did you need help?"

Kathryn worried her lower lip with her teeth, which he felt like her mouth against his sex, but he held himself in check.

"My mother was single when she had me," she said, and Luca blinked. He didn't know what he'd expected, but it wasn't that. Something so...mundane. "She'd never expected or even wanted to have a baby at all, but there she was, pregnant. Her partner made it clear he couldn't be bothered, and in case she'd any doubts about that, moved out of the country straightaway, so no one could expect him to contribute in any way to the life of a child he didn't want."

"He sounds charming."

Kathryn smiled, very slightly. "I wouldn't know. We've never met."

Luca watched as she moved to the bed and climbed onto the mattress, settling herself near the foot with her legs crossed beneath her and his shirt billowing around her slender form. It only made her look that much more fragile.

And made him want to protect her, somehow—even against this story she was telling him.

"My mother had huge dreams," she said after a moment. "She'd worked so hard to get where she was. She wanted a whole, rich life, and what she got instead was a daughter to raise right when she really could have made something of herself."

Something in the way she said that scraped at him. Luca frowned. "Surely raising a child is merely a different rich life. Not the lack of one altogether."

Kathryn's gaze met his for a moment then dropped.

"She'd worked so hard to succeed in finance, but couldn't keep up with the hours required once she had me. And once she left the job she loved, at an investment bank, she couldn't afford child care, so she had to manage it all on her own." She threaded her hands together in front of her. "All of my memories of her were of her working. She usually had more than one job, in fact, so I wouldn't want for anything. She wasn't too proud to do the things others refused to do. She cleaned houses on her hands and knees, anything to make my life better, and despite all of that, I was a terrible disappointment."

Luca had the sense that if he disputed this story, if he questioned it at all—and he couldn't understand why there was that thing in him that insisted this was a story that needed disputing when until hours ago he'd been Kathryn's biggest critic—she would stop talking. It was something in the set of her mouth, the line of her jaw. The stormy gray color of her eyes. So he said nothing. He merely exchanged his towel for a pair of exercise trousers and then crossed his arms over his chest. He waited.

Kathryn let out a breath that was more like a sigh.

"She wanted me to be an investment banker, too. That was always her preference, because she could teach me everything I needed to know and because her experience meant she could direct me."

"I believe that is called living through one's child. Not the best form of parenting, I think."

She frowned at him. "Not in this case. I could never get my head around the math. My mother tried to tutor me herself, but it was a waste of time. I can't think the way she can. My brain simply won't work the way hers does."

"My brain does not work the way my brother's does," Luca pointed out mildly, "and yet we've muddled along, running a rather successful company together for some time."

"That's different." Kathryn lifted a shoulder then dropped it. "I nearly killed myself getting a First in economics. I spent hours and hours torturing myself with the coursework. But I did it. Then I went on to an MBA course because that was what my mother thought was the best path toward the brightest future." She blew out a breath that made her fringe dance above her brow. "But the MBA was beyond torture. I was used to putting the hours in, but it wasn't enough. No matter what I did, it wasn't enough."

She shook her head, frowning down at her hands, and Luca had never wanted to touch another person more than he did then. She looked too small and something like defeated, and it lodged in his chest like a bullet.

It occurred to him that he'd never seen her look like this. That she'd fought him every step of the way, if sometimes only with a straight spine and a head held high. But *defeat* was not a word he'd ever associated with her before.

He found he hated it.

Kathryn met his gaze again then. "And that was when I met your father."

He shifted position and realized he was holding himself back as much as anything else. As if he didn't know what he might do if he stopped—as if he still had that little control, when it still involved Kathryn yet wasn't about sex. He couldn't say he much enjoyed the sensation.

But one great mess at a time, he thought darkly.

"Ah, yes," he said. "In that mythic waiting room, the birthplace of your epic friendship. The only friendship the old man ever had, as far as I am aware."

"You asked me to tell you this story," she pointed out. "You keep asking."

Luca couldn't trust himself to speak, one more novel

experience where this woman was concerned—and one he knew he would have to think about later. He inclined his head, silently bidding her to continue.

"It happened just as I told you," Kathryn said, her gaze reproving. "We started talking. Your father was charming. Funny."

Luca snorted. "Old."

"Maybe everyone is not as ageist as you are," she snapped at him.

He raked his hand through his hair then, annoyed and frustrated in equal measure.

"It is time for the truth, *cucciola mia*," he said then, roughly.

He moved before he knew he meant to, crossing over to place himself directly in front of her, at the foot of the high bed. She tilted up that chin of hers, as if she expected him to take a swing, and Luca was obviously deeply perverse, that such a thing should excite him. Or maybe it was simply that he liked it when she fought. When she stood up for herself, even against him. When she was nothing remotely like *defeated.*

"I'm telling you the truth. I can't help it if it's not the truth you want to hear." She eyed him, as if his proximity bothered her. Luca hoped it did. It would make them even. "I think we've already established that you have a history of believing what you want to believe, no matter what the actual truth might be."

He felt his mouth curve in acknowledgment. "But this is not a question of innocence. This is a question of how a young woman meets a much older man in a medical facility, so she could have no fantasy that there was anything virile about him at all, and decides to marry him anyway. I have no doubt that he proposed to you. That was what he did, always. But what made you agree?"

Kathryn held his gaze, and Luca didn't move. He didn't even blink, aware somehow that she was making a momentous decision. And he needed it to be the right one. *He needed it*—and he wasn't sure he wanted to investigate why that need was so intense. After a long while, she let out a sigh.

"My mother has crippling arthritis," Kathryn explained. "When it flares up she can hardly move. It had become very difficult for her to take care of herself." She shook her head, more as if she was shaking off a wave of emotion than negating anything. "I should have been there to help her, but between the classes for my degree and all the studying I had to do to barely keep up, I couldn't even do that well. I lived with her, which was one thing, but it was all beginning to feel a lot like drowning." She sucked in a breath. "But when my mother came out of her appointment, she recognized your father at a glance. One thing led to another, and we all went out for a meal."

Luca waited.

"Your father is very easy to talk to, actually."

"That was not a common sentiment."

"My mother told him everything. My struggles with my degree. Her battle with her arthritis. He was very kind." Her gray eyes grew distant, and he thought she tipped her chin up that much farther. "And at the end of the evening, he asked if he could see me—just me—again."

"This is where I think I need some clarification," Luca murmured. "Did you date a great deal?"

"I didn't date at all," she retorted, and he almost didn't

recognize that fierce thing that soared in him at that, possessiveness mixed with a kind of triumph.

"But you dated my father."

For the first time she looked uncomfortable. "I didn't necessarily want to *date* him," she said softly. "But he'd been so nice, and so sweet, and I didn't see the harm in having another dinner with him. I thought I was doing a good deed."

"What did your mother think?"

She didn't quite flinch. But he saw the tiny, abortive movement she made, and his eyes narrowed.

"She's always worried that I had more looks than sense," Kathryn said quietly. "Which I'm afraid I proved to her through my failures with my studies."

"A first-class degree is, by definition, not any kind of failure."

"I had to work ten times as hard as she did, and I still only did it by my teeth," she said with a dismissive wave of one hand. "But when we met your father, it seemed a perfect opportunity to stop worrying about the brains part and let the looks do some good for a change."

"What," Luca asked through his teeth, "does that mean?"

"It meant we both knew he liked the look of me," Kathryn said, with an edge to her voice. She sat up straighter on the bed. "And he was just as funny and kind and charming when I went out with him alone. Still, when he asked me to marry him on the third date, I laughed."

Her gaze had gone fierce. Protective, Luca thought.

"He told me that he knew he was a foolish old man, vain and silly, to think a young girl like me would want to shackle herself to a man like him. He knew he didn't have much time left. He assured me that all he wanted was companionship, because he didn't have any of the rest of it in him any longer. He told me I was the most beautiful thing he'd seen in years, and he couldn't think of a better way to go than to have me holding his hand."

"He flattered you."

"He *needed* me," she snapped. "He was old and scared and lonely. He told me that he had sons he wasn't close to and no particular reason to imagine that might change. He didn't want to die alone, Luca. I didn't think that made him a monster."

He felt as if he was nailed to the floor beneath him. As if he'd turned to stone.

"And this is why you married him? Out of pity? Out of the goodness of your heart? To save an old man from loneliness? You are a saint, indeed." Her breath hissed from her mouth. Luca kept going. "But he was a very wealthy man, Kathryn, and he did not traffic much in saints or pity. He didn't have to. He could have bought himself a fleet of nurses to keep him company, if company was what he wanted in his final days. So I'll ask you again. Why did he buy you?"

"He didn't buy me, Luca," she threw at him, sounding as furious as she did vulnerable. "He saved me."

Kathryn wanted to snatch the words back the moment she said them.

They hung there in the air between them, the glare of them enough to cast the rest of the room and even Luca in shadow.

She didn't know what she expected him to do, but it wasn't to simply stand there and gaze back at her, with all of his intensity focused hard on her, in a way she understood differently today.

The truth was, she understood a whole lot of things differently today.

Her own body. His body. The things he could *do* with both. What that look in his dark eyes meant—and more, what it had always meant, all these years, though she hadn't had a clue. Where it had always been leading them, this mad thing between them that not even the night they'd spent together had eased at all.

But she'd never said that out loud before, that little truth about her marriage. She wasn't entirely sure why she had now.

"Go on, then," Luca rumbled at her when it seemed whole ages had passed. When she'd died a thousand deaths, each one of them more disloyal than the last. "Explain that to me."

He stood there like some kind of ancient god of judgment, sculpted and remote, with his arms crossed and that mouth of his in a stern line. And it didn't seem to matter that he'd had that mouth on parts of her body she'd had no idea could be that sensitive. That he knew her now in a way no one else ever had. That he was the only person on the earth who had ever been *inside* her. It all made her dizzy.

And it didn't change the fact that he stared down at her as if he was hewn from rock. Or that compulsion she didn't understand that worked inside her, that wanted to give him anything he asked for, anything at all.

Anything. Even this.

"My mother was thrilled," she said, her voice scratchy, as if her own surrender choked her on its way down. "She got a cottage and her own live-in nurses out of the deal, so she never needs to work again."

Her mother had been something a bit more complicated than simply *thrilled*, Kathryn thought, though she didn't know how to explain that to this man. She didn't quite know how to think about it herself. All these years later.

"Being the wife of a man like Gianni Castelli is a full-time job," Rose had said imperiously, sitting at the kitchen table in their grotty old flat with the real-estate listings spread out before her. She'd had no doubt that Kathryn would accept Gianni's proposal. It hadn't even been a discussion. "It will require study and application, of course, should you want to make it into a career."

"A career?" Kathryn hadn't understood. "He's not well, Mum. He's not likely to last five years."

"You need to view this as an internship, my girl. A stepping stone to bigger and better things." Rose had eyed her up and down then shaken her head. "You're pretty enough, there's no denying it. And while you haven't proved to be as smart as we hoped, I'd imagine you can succeed in *this* arena anyway. The only figure you'll need to know is the size of your allowance."

"Mum," she'd said then, uncertainly. "I'm just not sure…"

"You listen to me, Kathryn," Rose had said, and she hadn't raised her voice. She hadn't needed to raise her voice, not when she used that withering tone. "I sacrificed everything for you. I worked myself into this state. And what would we have done if Gianni Castelli hadn't happened along and gone ass over teakettle for that face of yours? You need to capitalize on that." She'd sniffed. "For my sake, if nothing else. The truth is you've proved yourself unequal to the task of a career in finance. How will we pay the bills without this marriage?"

"But..." She'd felt all the usual things she always had when Rose spoke like this. Shame. Guilt. Despair that she was so deficient. Anguish that she couldn't live up to her mother's expectations. And that sliver of something else, something stubborn and forlorn, that didn't quite understand why nothing she did, no matter how hard she worked, was ever good enough. "It isn't *we*, Mum. It's me. I have to marry a man I don't love—"

"You must be having a laugh." Though the look on Rose's face had indicated there was precious little to laugh about. "Love? This isn't a fairy story, Kathryn. This is about duty and responsibility." She'd brandished her hands in the air, her gnarled and swollen knuckles. "Look at what I did to myself to do right by you. Look at how I ruined myself and threw away everything that ever mattered to me. It's between you and your conscience how you want to repay me."

And put that way, Kathryn hadn't had a choice.

"It sounds as if your mother got the better part of the bargain," Luca said quietly, snapping her back into the present.

"She got what she deserved after all she did for me," Kathryn said stoutly. "And I certainly couldn't give it to her. Thanks to your father, she can live out the rest of her days in peace. She's earned that."

There was a certain tightness to Luca's expression that suggested he didn't agree, and she tensed, instantly on the defensive, but he didn't pursue it. He cocked his head slightly to one side.

"And what did you earn?" he asked. "How did saving your mother save you?"

"I got to quit my MBA course," she said in a rush, and she felt the heat of that admission wash over her like some kind of flu. "I walked away and I never had to go back, and it didn't matter that we were out of the tuition money. The whole slate was wiped clean. All that struggle, all those years of never living up to expectations, gone in an instant and forgiven completely, simply because your father wanted to marry me."

And maybe, just maybe, she'd enjoyed a little holiday from her subservience to her mother's wishes. Maybe she'd liked having someone treat her like some kind of prize for a change.

"Kathryn," Luca said, his voice so gentle it made her shiver, "you must know—"

But she didn't want to hear whatever it was he was going to say. She didn't want whatever devastation that was lurking there in his dark eyes, lit now with something very much like compassion.

She lurched forward instead, coming up on her knees before him and throwing out her hands to catch herself against the wall of his chest. He didn't so much as rock on his feet with the impact. He simply studied her.

"Listen to me," Kathryn said, aware that she sounded desperate. "You can think whatever you like about your father's intentions. But to me, he was a dream come true. You don't have to like that," she said hurriedly when the edges of his mouth turned down, "but it's the truth. It's a fact."

And she was so close to him then. Touching him again. Her palms were propped against the sculpted perfection of his pectoral muscles, and that delirious heat of his poured into her, making her flush all over again.

But this fever she recognized.

Kathryn didn't want to talk about her marriage. She didn't want to talk about their complicated families. She didn't know what that dark thing was that lurked there in the way he was looking at her then, and she didn't want to know.

She did the only thing she knew to do. The only thing that made sense.

She tipped herself forward and pressed her mouth to his.

And it felt artless and silly, nothing like the way he'd kissed her—and for a shuddering moment that felt like forever he merely stood there, as if he was stunned—but then he moved. He took the back of her head in his palm and he opened his mouth, driving into hers and taking complete and delicious control.

He kissed her and he kissed her. He kissed her until she was wound around him, pressing herself against him, desperate and wild—because now she knew. Now she knew what else there was. Where else they could go.

All the magical things he could do.

But Luca pulled away, still curving that big hand of his over the back of her head, his dark eyes glittering.

"Did you do that to distract me?" he asked, his voice gruff. His breath not entirely steady—which made a whole different fire ignite within her.

"Yes," she said. Her mouth felt swollen again. And even though she wore his shirt and it covered more of her than some of her own clothes, she felt stripped bare. Naked and vulnerable and wide-open to him in every way.

"Is that the only reason?" If possible, his voice was even rougher.

Kathryn shifted on her knees. She slid her hands up,

over his jaw, holding his face between her palms, the way he'd done before to her. And she was so close that she could feel that shake in him, low and deep. So close she could feel that he was unsteady, too.

It made her feel as if she was made of light. As if she was filled with power.

"You might have noticed that I like kissing you, Luca," she said, and her voice was solemn. Because somehow everything between them had shifted, and there was something much too serious in his eyes. "You're my first."

"Your first in bed."

She waited, still holding him. She saw the exact moment he understood. The very second it crashed through him, leaving him stunned. And then something far darker, hungrier and indescribably male, lit him up. It made his dark eyes gleam. It made him tighten his grip.

"Cucciola mia," he murmured, his mouth against her lips, "we might kill each other."

And then he bore her back down to the bed and showed her exactly what he meant.

CHAPTER TEN

A WEEK LATER they concluded their business in California and flew back to Italy with Rafael, Lily and a private nurse for Lily and her unborn baby in tow.

Luca could have done without the crowd.

It had been a week of abject torture, having claimed Kathryn in private yet having to act as if nothing had changed between them in public. That she was the assistant he hadn't wanted, and he the Castelli who had always hated her the most. Luca had found that his much-vaunted control had deserted him almost entirely, making him uneasy about where this madness was leading him—but he couldn't stop.

Any moment of privacy they had, he exulted in her. Cars. Alcoves. Out walking the property. He kept waiting for this grip she had on him to ease, for the wildfire only she had ever stirred in him like this to abate—but it still hadn't. If anything, it grew stronger. Every day brighter and hotter than the day before.

It would be different once they were back in Rome, he told himself. There would be no sneaking around to avoid his brother, or at least, far less of that kind of thing. With no element of the forbidden, he was certain the hunger would ease. It always did. He was not the kind of man who formed attachments, and he knew better to want things he couldn't have. He'd learned that as a child, and he'd never forgotten it.

In truth, it had never been an issue before.

But first they had to make it to Rome, and separate themselves from his brother and Lily, who would be flying on to the family seat in the Dolomites. Several hours into their nighttime flight, only Rafael and Luca remained awake in the lounge area of the jet, the others having long since headed to the jet's stately guest rooms.

Rafael was talking about their next steps as a company and how best to capitalize on the goodwill they'd sown about the accounts in the wake of the annual ball. Luca, meanwhile, had spent longer than he cared to admit imagining Kathryn spread out against the pillows just down the plane's narrow hall, her long dark hair—

"Kathryn," Rafael said, intoning her name as if he could read Luca's dirty mind.

Luca eyed his brother across the width of the lounge and maintained his infinitely lazy position, stretched out on one of the couches like some kind of *dauphin*.

"Yes," he said. "Kathryn. My personal assistant, in fulfillment of our beloved patriarch's will. I haven't complained, have I?"

"You have not," his brother agreed. He looked so stern and austere as he sat there, his bearing far more dignified than Luca's had ever been. "That is what concerns me."

Luca forced a laugh he didn't feel. "I am nothing if not adaptable. And obedient."

"But that is the point." Rafael raised his brows. "You are neither one of those things, despite the great joy it gives you to pretend otherwise."

"You are mistaken, brother. I am nothing but a jumped-up playboy with excellent staff, all of whom are well paid to cover for my incompetence. The tabloids have decreed it, therefore it must be true."

Rafael said nothing for a moment that dragged on too long. Luca found himself clenching his jaw and forced himself to stop.

"I expected you to run her off within the week."

Luca shrugged. "She proved somewhat more tenacious than anticipated."

Rafael considered him. "She was also a surprising asset these past two weeks. The accounts adored her. I suspect half of them raced to the tabloids to submit their own *Saint Kate* stories within hours of meeting her." He stretched his legs out before him. "Needless to say, this has put a rather positive spin on things. I had more business associates than I can count commend me—us—on our magnanimity in hiring her. She might as well be the mascot of the company."

Luca didn't remember moving, but there he was, sitting up and glaring at his older brother.

"This is a temporary situation," he said, his voice clipped. "We agreed on that."

"Maybe we should reconsider." Rafael shrugged when Luca continued to glare at him. "If using Saint Kate boosts our profile, I don't see why we *wouldn't* use her as long as possible."

"Perhaps," Luca said coolly, "the lady no longer wishes to be used. It's possible she had her fill of it during her commercial transaction of a marriage. Maybe all she wants to do is her job."

That was, of course, a huge mistake. He knew it the moment he spoke without thinking—as it was the first time he could remember doing so to a family member since he was a child.

Rafael blinked. "I don't care what she wants, as long as it benefits the company," he said in a low voice.

"The company," Luca muttered, again without thinking. Almost as if he couldn't control himself at all. "Always the company."

He didn't much care for the way his brother looked at him then.

"Have our objectives changed without my knowledge, Luca?" Rafael let that sit there for a moment, and the expression on his face was far too shrewd for Luca's peace of mind. "Have yours?"

It was not until she was safely barricaded in her little Italian flat that Kathryn really breathed.

And moments after that first, deep, full-bodied breath, she simply sank down on the soft carpet in her cozy lounge, as if the knees that had somehow carried her all the way through her trip to California and the long flight back were no longer up to the task. As if everything that had happened in the past two weeks finally caught up with her.

With a wallop.

She found herself looking around her flat, the morning light streaming in from the high windows that had sold her on the place, as if she'd never seen it before. It was hard to imagine the person she'd been when she'd left here. The person she'd left behind her in Sonoma somewhere.

How could her whole world change so quickly?

Her marriage to Gianni had been a change, certainly, but it had been a change of circumstances, not of who she was inside. She had merely swapped one set of duties and obligations for another, and the truth was, she'd found caring for Gianni infinitely more pleasant than statistics. Or tending to her difficult mother, if she was brutally honest with herself.

This was different. *She* was different.

And she had no idea if she needed to set about putting herself back together somehow, or if she needed to figure out a way to simply accept who she'd become. Whoever the hell that was.

Kathryn breathed in, deep. Then out again. She did it a few more times, and then she climbed back to her feet and decided that a cup of tea was all the answer she needed just now. Everything else would wait.

She was just finishing that same cup, sitting out on her small balcony with her view over the red-tipped Roman rooftops that made her heart sing a little in her chest, when she heard the banging on her front door.

Luca, she thought at once. Because who else could it be?

And the fact that her heart echoed that pounding told her more than she needed to know about those feelings that the tea hadn't suppressed at all.

She considered not answering it—but dismissed that thought in an instant. This was Luca. It wasn't as if he'd simply shrug and wander off.

Kathryn padded to the door in her bare feet and swung it open, not at all surprised to find him braced there against the doorjamb, one arm over his head and a scowl on his face.

"Where did you go?" he demanded.

"Home," she replied. "Obviously."

He ignored that. "Why did you race off like that? I looked around and you'd disappeared."

She didn't want to let him inside her flat, and she couldn't have said why. She crossed her arms over her chest and stood in the doorway instead.

"I came home," she said, very distinctly. "You told me I didn't have to go into work today. Has something changed?"

Something ignited in those dark eyes of his, and he pushed himself off the doorjamb. Technically, he'd moved back, and yet he still seemed to fill the doorway. The narrow hallway behind him. The whole of her flat he hadn't even entered.

"What do you think is happening here, Kathryn?" he asked softly.

She refused to show him her uncertainty. That had been situational, she assured herself. She'd lost her virginity to this man, and he was a very demanding, very detail-oriented lover. Anyone would have trouble finding her footing after that kind of combination.

But she was standing just fine now.

"What's happening is that after a long, two-week business trip, my boss is standing at my door," she said crisply. "If you don't have an assignment for me, I think you should leave."

She expected his temper, braced herself for it. Luca looked astounded for a beat, but then, impossibly, he laughed. And it was that same delighted, beautiful laugh of his that rivaled the Italian scenery itself and did far worse things to her poor heart. It made her scowl at him, so determined was she to ward him off. To keep that laughter from sinking in deep beneath her skin.

But it was like fighting off sunlight. No matter what she wanted, no matter what she did, it filled her.

"Come here, *cucciola mia*," he said when the laughter faded away.

He crooked his finger at her, and she wanted to bite him. He was a foot away at most. He was already too close.

"I'm right here," she told him. "I don't need to come any closer, and I'm not your pet."

"That's where you're wrong," he said in that dark voice of his that made need roll through her like a terrible thirst. "Come, Kathryn. Put that mouth on me. It will feel much better than using it as a battering ram when I can see you don't mean it."

"I do."

"You do not," he corrected her. He moved toward her then, advancing on her with that intense gleam in his dark gaze that she knew now was hunger. And the remains of that laughter that made him seem even more beautiful than he already was. "You're afraid."

"I most certainly am not," she said, but then she couldn't move any farther.

He'd backed her up into her flat and straight into the wall of the small foyer, and she hadn't even noticed. She swallowed, hard.

"I'm not afraid," she told him, very distinctly. "But I need some time to clear my head."

"Why?"

"I don't have to justify how I spend my free time to you."

"You don't. But you could spend it beneath me, driving us both insane with the way you move those hips of yours. You can see why I'd agitate for that option."

Her jaw worked, but no words came out. Luca grinned.

"We can't just…have sex all the time," she protested, but even she could hear that her voice was weak. Reedy.

This time that marvelous laughter stayed in his eyes, making them gleam gold and shiver straight through her.

"Why ever not?"

"Sex is a weakness," she told him, very seriously, the words coming from some part of her she hadn't known was there. "A weapon."

"That sounds like the ravings of someone who isn't very good at it, *cucciola mia*, and therefore doesn't enjoy it," he said with another laugh, obviously unaware that he'd just dismissed one of her mother's favorite sayings so easily. "A description that does not fit you at all."

She didn't know what expression she wore then, but his hard face softened, and he pulled her against him as if she was a fragile little thing, made of spun glass. He smoothed her hair back from her face, as she'd already discovered he loved to do. And when he gazed down at her there was something so bright in his eyes that it made her shake.

And her heart broke open inside her, telling her things she didn't want to accept. Making her feel things she'd never thought she'd feel for anyone, and certainly not for him. But she might have been a virgin before she'd met Luca, and she might have been completely untouched until he'd handled that, too, but she wasn't an idiot.

Only an idiot would tell Luca Castelli she was falling in love with him, she scolded herself. *He doesn't want to know.*

"I can't think around you," she whispered, though she knew she shouldn't. That it was far too close to a truth even she wanted to pretend wasn't real. "Sex only makes it worse."

She felt his chest move against her as if he was laughing, though he didn't make a sound. Slowly, slowly, his perfect mouth curved.

"I know," he said, and he ran his hands down the length of her spine, then over the curves of her bottom, pulling her flush against him. "Sex makes everything terrible."

He was hot and hard against her belly, and she thought he knew the precise moment when she simply... melted. Kathryn thought he always knew.

Luca smiled then. "But then it makes it much, much better."

And when he set about proving it, Kathryn surrendered.

Because she wanted him more than she wanted to resist him.

And she thought he knew that, too.

Some ten days after their return from California, Luca paused at his office door after finishing a round of calls to the States and frowned. It was late in the evening, and his staff had long since departed for the day—all except Kathryn.

She sat at her desk in the open space outside his office, where she was meant to act as his guard and first line of support, furiously typing—which didn't make any sense. He hadn't given her any work that needed finishing at this hour.

"You should have left hours ago," he said, and the beast that still paced inside him when it came to her growled in approval when she jolted at the sound of his voice, then melted into a smile. "Didn't I mention something about swimming naked beneath the stars? That happens upstairs, Kathryn. Away from the computer."

"I have to finish this," she said, her fingers flying over the keys. "Then we can stargaze all you like."

"It's the naked part that interests me, *cucciola mia.* The stars are a ploy. You may not have noticed this, but we're in the middle of the city."

She wrinkled her nose at him, which he found tugged at him in ways that he wasn't entirely comfortable exploring, but she typed on. He moved to stand behind her, smoothing his hands over her shoulders and tugging gently on the end of her fashionably sleek ponytail. She sighed happily enough, but she didn't stop, and he read over her shoulder.

And this time, he scowled. "This is Marco's report. He told me he'd have it in to me tomorrow morning."

"And so he will," Kathryn said, her voice even. "Just as soon as I finish it."

Luca pulled her chair back from the desk, forcing her to stop, then swiveled it around so he could look her in the eyes. Hers were gray and far too calm when they met his.

"You are not Marco's assistant," he told her, perhaps more harshly than necessary. "You are mine."

Kathryn was far more than that, though Luca knew he didn't have the words to tell her that. She was that pounding in his heart. She was that heat that never left him. And all of that was wrapped up in those cool gray eyes, that serene little smile, the entire package that was Kathryn. *His.*

"Perhaps you're unaware that it's part of your assistant's job to pretty up all the reports that make it to your desk," Kathryn said mildly.

"It is not."

"How strange," she murmured. "I have been assured by no less than six different members of the team that it is."

Of course she'd been told that—and who knew what else? He'd essentially declared open season on her when he'd brought her on board. How had he managed to forget that? But of course, he knew how. Because all he thought about was getting his hands on her—and she never, ever complained. She smiled instead.

He shoved his hair back with an impatient hand. "I will speak to them."

"No," she countered, "you will not."

"They cannot continue to abuse you in this fashion."

She leaned back in her chair and crossed her arms. "You can't interfere. It will work itself out."

"This is not a cause worth martyring yourself for," he told her. "I put this target on your back. I'll take it off."

"And if you do that, you might as well shoot me yourself," she said, with an edge to her voice. "I don't need you to give me special treatment. Everyone knows you were forced to hire me. You stepping in now will only make it worse."

"Kathryn—"

"I told you I'd be good at this and I am," she said, her voice low and her chin high. "My work speaks for itself. It will win over your team, and if it doesn't, doing all the work they don't want to do means I'll know their jobs as well as mine. It all only helps me."

"You don't need any help."

"I couldn't do the job I trained my whole life to do,"

she threw at him fiercely. And he knew she meant the job her mother had wanted for her. "This is my chance. I'm not going to waste it, and I'm not going to let you save me, either. I'll succeed or fail on my own."

He stared down at her, a kind of battle inside him that he didn't understand. Maybe he didn't want to understand it. Maybe what was shaking through him was so outside his experience, understanding the truth of it might break him in two.

"You let my father save you once," he said quietly.

She didn't flinch from that. She held his gaze, though he could feel the way it burned, and hers was solemn.

"And now I want to save myself," she said with soft determination. "And I want you to let me."

CHAPTER ELEVEN

ANOTHER WEEK EASED BY, then another, and Luca was forced to face the fact that his driving need for Kathryn wasn't going anywhere.

He'd spent more time with her than any other woman he'd ever been with. She worked with him. She traveled with him. She slept with him. He would have imagined that such familiarity could only breed the swiftest contempt, but Kathryn was a revelation. Daily. She fascinated him, from her cool competence in the office that even his staff had been forced to heed to her uninhibited delight in all they did together in bed.

It was too perfect. Too good. And he had learned the hard way that there was no such thing as "too good to be true." There was only paying for it.

His childhood had taught him well.

He remembered it all too vividly, the various ways he'd acted out in the vain hope of getting his father's attention. The commotion he'd caused. The precious objects he'd broken. The tantrums, the running away, the back talk. All so someone who was actually related to him would show him that they'd cared about him—but that had never happened.

And Luca was no longer an abandoned boy. He'd

long since forgiven his brother, who had handled their family situation in the best way he'd known how—and had then embroiled himself in a mad relationship with Lily. His mother had killed herself—he didn't care that the hospital had claimed it had been an accident, he'd never doubted what she'd done—rather than face the children she'd made. And Gianni had never paid the slightest attention to Luca. His heir apparent had been one thing, but Luca had merely been the forgotten spare.

He didn't know how to believe in the possibility that Kathryn could truly want him. That she'd chosen him to work with. That all of this wasn't a giant ploy.

"What reaction are you looking for?" one of his stepmothers had asked him years ago, when Luca had broken all the dishes at dinner one night. Gianni had merely exited the room, as if Luca was an animal far beneath his notice. His stepmother had remained, brittle and cold.

"I hate you," Luca had shouted at her, with all the fury in his ten-year-old heart.

"No one hates you," she'd replied, her gaze bland on his. "No one cares either way. The sooner you recognize that, the happier you'll be."

He'd never forgotten it. And he'd never begged for attention again.

Today was a lazy Sunday that hinted of spring. He breathed it in, hard. He'd woken Kathryn in his usual fashion while it was still dark, left her quivering in his bed and had gone out for a long run around his beautiful city while it was still shaking off the last of the night before. He ran through piazzas that were famed for their crowds, past famous fountains and monuments, all deserted this early in the day, as if Rome was entirely his.

He was waiting for the other shoe to drop and crush him where he stood. He told himself he expected it, so it couldn't possibly be too bad. Even if he couldn't quite imagine what that might be. He ran faster. Harder.

It was his favorite time to run, these early mornings that were all his. He usually took his time, doing lazy loops through places usually too packed to navigate. But he found that today, knowing Kathryn waited in his penthouse for his return, he ran even faster on his way back home.

She wasn't on the first level of the penthouse when he returned, as she often was, usually making coffee or putting together something to eat in his kitchen. He climbed the spiral stairs from his vast living area up to his rooftop bedroom, expecting to find her still sprawled in his bed. But that was empty, too, the duvet tossed back and the pillows still dented.

Luca peered out through the windows and saw her on the farthest part of the roof, her back to him, her eyes on the city laid out at her feet. He took a quick detour into his bathroom, showering off his run, then pulled on the pair of trousers he'd left at the foot of the bed before he went outside.

She didn't turn as he closed the great glass door behind him, or even when he skirted the pool. She stayed as she was, her back perhaps *too* straight, he thought, as he drew close.

"I hope you're not thinking of jumping," he said as he came up behind her. "I would not find that amusing at all." Kathryn didn't respond, not even when he came to stand beside her at the balustrade. She looked pale. Almost…scared, he would have said, if she'd been anyone else. If that made any sense. "Has something happened?"

She swallowed, and he saw she was hugging herself, wrapped up tight in one of the draped sweaters she preferred, as if she needed armor. Slowly, much too slowly, she turned to face him.

"I don't know how to tell you this," she said, and even her voice didn't sound like hers.

Her eyes were dark gray, the darkest he'd ever seen them. Her lovely mouth was pressed into a vulnerable line. And when Luca reached out to touch her face, she jerked away.

"I suggest you do it fast," he said, frowning, as something cold washed over him.

She looked lost for a moment. Then she seemed to collect herself.

"After you left," she said, still in that strangely disembodied voice, as if she was speaking to him from a great distance, "I was sick."

"Then, what are you doing out here?" he demanded, a protective impulse he hadn't known he possessed roaring inside him. "Come. We'll put you back in bed."

"I've had this strange stomach thing for a while now," she told him, not moving at all. "It comes and goes. I thought maybe it was anxiety." He waited. Sheer misery washed over her face, and she pressed her lips together, hard, as if she was holding back a sob. "But today something else occurred to me. So I went to the supermarket and I got a test. And I had my answer in an instant."

Luca felt as if he'd been frozen solid where he stood.

He was aware of everything. The breeze with its

hints of spring that danced between them and toyed with her hair. The way the old gold of the sun made the city gleam all around them. The clatter of traffic in the distance and bells ringing out on the wind.

And the thing she was about to say, that made all of this—all he'd felt and all that had happened since that night in the car in California—a lie. A scam. That other shoe he'd been expecting all this time, kicking him straight in the face. The ultimate act of a creature who had deceived him completely, snowed him utterly. Made him believe he could be a different man. Made him imagine for an instant that he could live a different life. Made him forget all the truths he knew about this one.

But he had always known better. He had never given up his control, not ever, until her. He had never begged for anyone's attention. He had never wanted a damned thing.

And this was why.

Luca thought what he would find most unforgivable when the dust cleared was that even now, even in this sharp, unbearable instant when he understood exactly how expertly he'd been played for a fool, he would have given anything at all for her to say something else.

Anything else.

Anything that would allow him to keep pretending he could be this other, softer version of himself—

But that was not his fate.

And she was an illusion.

He should have known that from the start.

Even then, he hoped. God, how he hoped.

"Luca," she said, his name in her mouth like a blow. The final betrayal in a war he hadn't realized she'd been fighting all this while. A war he understood, at last, he'd lost the moment he'd stopped viewing her as his enemy, when she'd never been anything but. *Never.* And that meant he would hurt her in any way he could. In every way. "I'm pregnant."

Kathryn found she was clenching her hands together in front of her, and she couldn't seem to stop it, no matter how revealing that was. No matter that the man she'd fallen in love with despite herself had gone so still he could have been part of the stone wall that surrounded his rooftop terrace. Just another Roman statue, and about as approachable.

She didn't know what she expected. Luca to grow pale. To shout. To keel over or stagger about dramatically. To react in some over-the-top and awful way, as she'd imagined he would and had braced herself against—because she'd spent a deeply unpleasant hour or so since she'd taken that test imagining all the various horrible ways Luca might take this news, and panicking about each and every one of them in turn.

He did none of those things.

Instead, he stared.

His gaze dropped from her face to her belly, where he should know perfectly well there would be no sign of anything. Not this soon. It took him a long time to drag that dark gaze of his back up. He stared at her far past the point where it could be considered anything but aggressive, while a muscle clenched in his lean jaw, and every nerve in Kathryn's body tied itself into a painful knot.

And yet when Luca finally spoke, his voice was something like lazy. Ripe with disinterest and bland insult.

She recognized that voice instantly. She'd forgotten how much she hated it.

"You have the necessary paperwork, I assume, to support this claim."

Kathryn blinked. "Paperwork? I took a pregnancy test. It's a…stick, not paper."

Luca's dark eyes gleamed, and not in a nice way.

"Kathryn, please," he said, with a little laugh that was like sandpaper against her skin. "Surely you cannot imagine that you are the first woman to share my bed and then decide she'd quite like to nurse at the Castelli teat for the rest of her life." He shrugged. Horribly. "I like sex, as you have discovered, and in these things there is always risk. I would never dismiss a paternity claim out of hand." His dark gaze hurt as it bored into her. "But I do insist that it be proved beyond any doubt."

She realized her hands had balled into fists. "Do you have a great many accidental children, then?"

"I have none, in fact," Luca said viciously. As if he meant it to be a blow. "Such is the perfidy of the average woman."

"You mean the average woman you choose to sleep with," Kathryn threw at him, because she couldn't seem to help herself. When he'd left this morning to go on his run she'd been toying with the idea of telling him how she felt, because it was so huge, so overwhelming, she didn't think she could keep it to herself. Now she rather thought she'd prefer to die. "Maybe the common denominator is less their treachery and more you."

He eyed her from his place a foot or so away with that same searing fury and simmering dislike that had always made her feel…restless before. When she hadn't known him. When she hadn't understood what that thing was between them.

Now it simply made her feel sick.

"I will assemble the usual team of lawyers and doctors," Luca said, sounding deeply bored. "I'll inform them you'll be in tomorrow for the typical workup." Despite that tone, there wasn't a trace of boredom in the searing fury of those dark eyes of his. Not the faintest hint. "Does that suit your schedule? You'll have a great deal of free time, if that helps. My father's will means I can't fire you, but I think you'll find you'll work better as a distant telecommuter from here on out."

"I…" Kathryn shook her head again, refusing to succumb to the wave of dizziness that buffeted her. She shouldn't have been surprised by this, either. When had she ever had the upper hand with Luca? Why had she foolishly held out some kernel of hope that he'd react better? She hadn't realized *how much* she'd been holding on to that hope until now, she realized. When he'd crushed it. "But…"

"I'm sorry if this does not live up to your fantasies of melodrama, *Stepmother*," he said, his voice like steel and that word as harsh as if he'd backhanded her with it. Kathryn fell back a step as if he really had. "You should be aware that eighty percent of the women who make these claims do not return for the appointment that would prove them liars. The other twenty percent must imagine that I'm kidding when I say I'll run these tests. I'm not. Which will you be, I wonder?"

Kathryn felt off balance and worse, something like half hollow, half sick. And beyond that, she had the sickening sense that this had all happened before. Not to her, but because of her. Her own mother had been forced to have a conversation just like this one. Kathryn, too, had been an accident. She found she couldn't get her head around that—it was too much déjà vu to take in at once.

But one thing was perfectly clear. She'd failed her mother. Again. And this time, in the one way she knew Rose could never forgive. That was fair enough. Kathryn was quite sure she'd never forgive herself, either.

"Luca," she said, and she didn't care that her voice shook, that her eyes were blurry with tears, "you don't have to do this."

He laughed. The derisive note in it scraped at her, as she supposed it was meant to do. "Your acting skills are impressive, Kathryn. Maybe far more impressive than I realized."

Her teeth ached. She realized she was gritting them. "You know perfectly well I was a virgin."

"I know that's what you wanted me to think," he threw back at her, his tone mild and unperturbed, though his eyes blazed. "But who can say what is true and what is one more bit of theater from one such as you? A DNA test is far more straightforward."

She shook her head at him, furious with herself that she was so susceptible to him. Furious that he always won. *Always.*

Furious that despite everything, she'd forgotten that deep down, this man hated her. Everything else was sex. The truth was that Luca had always hated her and always would. And they'd made a child out of that. Out of her profound stupidity in the face of the one temptation she hadn't denied herself.

It only takes one mistake, her mother had always told her.

And Kathryn had made it. But that didn't mean she

had to make another one. She'd told Luca she wanted to save herself. Now she had someone else to think about, and the best thing she could do for her baby was keep it the hell away from Luca Castelli and all that hate that burned in him like coals and never, ever went out.

It didn't matter that she thought she loved him. Maybe she did. But what mattered was what kind of life she could provide for the baby she carried. That swept over her with all the grace and conviction of a plan, as if this hadn't been a mistake at all. As if she'd made this decision instead of having it thrust upon her.

Kathryn supposed it didn't matter either way. None of this mattered. Someday her child would tell the story of his or her father with a shrug, just as Kathryn did, and the world would go right on turning.

Her broken heart didn't matter to anyone. It never had.

She cleared her throat and got on with it. "Let me make this simple, then," she said, pleased her voice sounded, if not quite even, like hers again. "I quit. I'll contact Rafael and let him know I'd prefer the bulk sum your father left me, and you'll never see me again. Are you happy now?"

If possible, his gaze got darker. More intense. The blast of his temper scorched her, the fire of it crowding her as if it had eaten the whole of Rome alive, the flames licking over her skin. She braced herself as if she expected him to haul off and hit her, because his gorgeously elegant fingers curled up into fists right there at his sides—

But he didn't hit her. Of course he didn't hit her.

That would have been easier to bear.

Instead, Luca reached over, curled a hard hand around her neck and hauled her mouth to his.

He tasted like sin and redemption, fury and betrayal, and Kathryn was a fool.

An inexcusable fool, but she couldn't stop kissing him back. Even if this was the last time.

Or especially because it was the last time.

He angled his jaw, taking her mouth as if he owned her, and the burn of it flooded through her. He hauled her even closer, so her breasts were crushed against his chest, and she arched into him despite herself.

Her heart kicked at her, a wild and desperate drumming.

He sank his hands into her hair and he devoured her, kissing her again and again. Until she was pliant against him. Until she was kissing him back with the same wildfire, the same mindless need.

And only then did he let her go.

"Luca…" she whispered.

But his face twisted with dislike and disillusion, and something so harsh it made her stomach ache.

"Get out," he told her, in a stranger's pitiless voice that rocked through her like a terrible hurricane, destroying everything in its path. She knew she'd bear the mark of it forever, her own, secret scar. "And, Kathryn…"

She waited, unable to see through the misery that clouded her eyes. Aware that she was trembling, and not sure she'd ever stop. The look he gave her ripped her apart, but when he spoke, his voice was arctic.

"Don't come back here. Ever."

Three days later, Luca was seething his way through a meeting in his conference room when every mobile phone in his office blew up with texts and calls.

His particularly.

He grimly ignored it, gesturing for the man in front of him to continue his presentation. But as the meeting droned on, he saw entirely too much activity on the other side of the glass. His mobile kept buzzing.

And finally, his senior PR person came and stood at the door with an expression on her face that boded nothing but ill.

"Excuse me," Luca said. "It appears I am needed."

He swiped his mobile from the tabletop and stepped out into the office, scowling at Isabella.

"What is it?"

"Ah, well." She actually backed away from him. "The tabloids. I think you'd better look."

He refused to think her name, even though it burst through him then like a song. He felt that like another betrayal. His mobile vibrated in his hand, but he didn't glance at it. Not with every person in his office trying so hard not to stare at him.

He made his way toward his office, past her empty desk that he hadn't been able to make himself fill yet because she'd ruined him, she truly had, and he closed himself inside.

He went to his computer to find his inbox full. Gritting his teeth, he clicked on the links that so many people had helpfully sent him. And there it was.

SAINT KATE IN SEX ROMP WITH GIANNI'S PLAYBOY SON!
SAINT KATE UPGRADES FROM FATHER TO SON!
SAINT KATE STEPMAMA DRAMA!

And underneath the shrieking headlines were the pictures. Kathryn on his roof. More to the point, Luca on his roof with her, half-naked, kissing her as if his life depended on it. As if she hadn't just revealed herself as the traitorous, mercenary bitch she was. As if that wasn't a scene of desperation and betrayal, and nothing more.

Next to him, his mobile buzzed again, this time with a text from Rafael.

Fix it, it read.

It was succinct and to the point, and did nothing at all to soothe the raging thing inside Luca that was too angry, too ferocious to be a simple beast. This thing wanted blood. This thing wanted payback.

This time, he vowed, he wouldn't rest until he'd destroyed her, too.

CHAPTER TWELVE

KATHRYN NOTICED THE sleek black luxury car, entirely too flashy for the quiet English country lane it blocked, the moment she came around the bend on her walk back from the shops.

It had been twelve days since she'd dragged herself out of Rome and back to England. Twelve days since she'd gotten on the next flight back home. She'd never been so pleased to return to her native Yorkshire in all her life. The wolds and the country lanes. The clouds and the green. The redbrick houses that lined this small village, just over five miles outside Hull's city center.

Even her prickly mother, she told herself, was a vast improvement over anyone named Castelli.

She slowed her pace as she drew closer to the car, parked as it was at a sharp angle directly in front of the cottage. Her carrier bag *thwacked* against her thigh. High above, plump clouds scudded across the winter sky, some thick with rain, some as wispy as cotton.

And then Luca threw open the low-slung driver's door and climbed out, unfolding himself onto her remote little lane like a nightmare come to life.

A nightmare, she told herself firmly, as her heart squeezed tight in her chest. *Definitely a nightmare.*

She couldn't pretend she was entirely surprised. She'd seen all the papers. So had everyone else in this tiny little village—and most of England, for that matter. To say nothing of all the world.

Kathryn had told herself that if she could weather a tabloid storm in a village this small, she could do anything. Including having a second generation of illegitimate children, like her mother before her. She'd imagined that when her pregnancy eventually became impossible to conceal, it would seem unworthy of comment in comparison.

"It's like you to give up, isn't it?" her mother had sniffed when Kathryn had made it home. "I think we both know that's your father's blood in you. Making you as weak as he was."

There'd been no point replying to that. Or to the far more unkind things Rose had said when the tabloids had splashed those pictures everywhere.

She'd decided that was all fine, too. She could stomp around in the chilly Yorkshire lanes wrapped up in concealing coats and heavy boots and pretend she was invisible, until she wasn't.

Luca, by contrast, looked lethal. Not invisible at all. He wore a pair of casual trousers and a shirt that would have looked unremarkable on any of the men Kathryn had just seen down on the high street, but this was Luca. He somehow looked as powerful, as darkly ruthless, as he had when he'd been wearing a bespoke suit. His hair was in its usual tousled state that somehow softened the austere male beauty of his hard face, making him that much more stunning. And no matter that he was scowling at her.

The difference was that today Kathryn didn't give a toss. He couldn't break what was already broken.

What he'd stomped into pieces himself on that rooftop far away.

"Oh, lovely," she said coolly as she drew closer. She didn't smile at him, not even a forced rendition of one, and she told herself it was a bit sad that felt like a rebellion. "Does this mean it's my turn to fling horrid accusations at your head and shred your character at will? I've been saving up insults, just in case."

"You took your turn in the tabloids," he bit out. "So here I am, and no matter that it took me over a week to track you down to this godforsaken place. What do you want?"

Kathryn blinked. "I don't want anything. I might have liked some compassion when I told you some startling news, but that ship sailed."

"What game is this?" His voice was soft, but Kathryn could hear the thunder in it. It rolled off him like electricity and deep into her, setting off a different set of explosions. "What can you possibly hope to win?"

Kathryn shifted her weight back on her heels and studied him, shoving her hands deep into her coat pockets as she did. He looked...unhinged, she thought. She'd never seen that wild look in Luca's dark eyes, nor that tension that seemed to grip him.

Luca slammed the car door shut with more violence than was necessary, rocking the magnificent sports car where it sprawled there, as muscular and dangerous as he was. Kathryn thought he might reach for her then, and braced herself against it—but he only eyed her in that predatory way of his that made her blood feel spiked in her veins.

Then he leaned back against the car, crossing one boot over the other and his arms over his chest as if he was not only wholly at his ease, but also impervious to the Yorkshire winter wind that whipped down the lane in irregular bursts to shake the trees and slap at them. As if he would stand there forever if she didn't answer him.

"I don't want anything from you." Kathryn met his dark gaze and felt that same old heavy, edgy thing flip over deep inside her. Maybe she would always have this odd yearning, this bizarre hope that he might prove himself a different man. But he wasn't. And she didn't have to tolerate the way he spoke to her. "I told you that you're going to be a father. What you choose to do with that information is entirely up to you."

"And this independent stance has nothing to do with the fact that if I fail to claim this child you can try to pass it off as my father's, I'm sure." Luca's eyes blazed, though he still stood there as if he was relaxed. "And in so doing, potentially win yourself a conservatorship of one-third of the Castelli fortune my brother and I now share between us. That is quite the luxurious life you've plotted out for yourself, *Stepmother.* Let me guess. You spent your entire marriage trying to get pregnant, but failed. Then when my father died, you realized you had one shot left. Rafael has never had eyes for any woman but Lily, not even when he thought she was dead, which left me."

She wished she could run him over with his own ridiculous car.

"Right," she said in a flat voice. "You've figured me out. Except for the fact that I was a virgin, as you know very well."

"There are words for what you are," he retorted, in that hard-edged way that slapped at her the same way it had in Rome. "But I don't think *virgin* is one of them."

"Yes," she said, scathingly. "You saw to that."

"You can't lose, can you?" He was seething, she realized. So furious that the only thing containing him was the way he held himself there, so rigid and still. "If I do nothing, the way I would with any other woman who tried to claim I'd impregnated her, the world will assume the child is my father's. You've guaranteed yourself a payday for the rest of your mercenary little life."

Kathryn opened her mouth to throw something back at him, to defend herself somehow, but instead found herself swamped by a tide of heavy emotion, as deep and as dark as the North Sea. She tried to fight it off. She'd sworn to herself that this man would never see her cry again, that he didn't deserve it—

But it was no use.

It rushed over her. It betrayed her as surely as he had.

Entirely against her will, Kathryn sobbed.

All the things he'd called her over these past two years, and the past twelve days in particular. All those vicious lies in the paper. All the nasty things her mother had said to her about history repeating itself, but much dumber this time. And the way Luca had turned on her so completely. So certain she was every terrible thing she'd been called.

So certain that he'd called her some of them himself, this same man who had tended to her so gently that night in Sonoma. Held her against him and bathed her himself.

She sobbed and she sobbed.

"How could you?" she demanded, when she could

talk—or try—through the flood of tears. "You were there, Luca. You know perfectly well this baby is nobody's but yours!"

"Why?" he threw right back at her, and he wasn't standing there so languidly any longer. He didn't sound like himself, either. Not lazy or amused in the least. He moved toward her, wrapping his hands around her upper arms and pulling her face to his. "You held on to your virginity against all odds for twenty-five years, even made it through an entire marriage with it intact, then threw it away in the back of a car with a man who used to be your stepson? Why would anyone do that without an ulterior motive? How could it be anything but a plot?"

Kathryn shook with all the huge and unwieldy things inside her. She didn't know when she'd dropped the carrier bag. Or when she started pounding her fists against his impervious chest.

"Because I love you, you jackass!" she cried.

He closed his hands over her fists and held them away from him, and something in the expression on his beautiful face made her still. She stopped trying to hit him. She stopped fighting. All she could hear was her own ragged breathing, and everything else was that raw thing in his eyes.

And the foolishness in her, that still hurt when he did.

"Then, you are the only one who ever has," Luca said, matter-of-fact and quiet.

And it turned out a broken heart could break again, after all.

Luca felt outside himself. He let go of Kathryn's hands, and she wiped at her face. And he didn't understand how he could feel turned inside out, a stranger to himself, and still enjoy it when she straightened and fixed him with that fierce scowl of hers.

Had he really come here to hurt her? He'd been lying to himself. He understood that he'd have taken any excuse at all to hunt her down. Any reason in the world to see her again. Anything to shift this darkness off him—and only she could do that, though Luca couldn't think of a single reason in the world she'd want to do anything of the kind.

"That's ridiculous," she said crossly now. "Of course you're loved. The whole world loves you. You are beloved wherever you go."

"I am known. It's not the same thing."

"Your family—"

"Listen to me," Luca said, his voice darker than he meant it to be and far more urgent. "My father loved his money and his search for new wives. My mother loved her own illness. Rafael loves Lily. I decided early on that I wanted no part of any of that, because there was no room for me anyway. I wanted control, not love. I wanted to make sure nothing and no one could hurt me the way all of them either hurt others or were hurt themselves. Maybe the truth is I don't know how. It isn't in me."

Her scowl deepened. "Luca—"

"And then came you," he gritted out. "You got under my skin from the first. You spent two years married to my father and still, you drove me crazy. I've never met anyone who bothered me more."

"You've mentioned that. At length."

"But I couldn't stay away from you, Kathryn. I couldn't stop." He shook his head. "And then, when I touched you, I didn't want to stop. I thought that maybe I'd finally found the thing that brought down every other member of my family. I thought maybe I could be different." He blew out a breath. "Then you betrayed me, and I knew."

Her gray eyes were dark and solemn. "You knew what?"

"That it's no more than what I deserve," he said harshly. "I don't blame you for wanting to do this on your own. You shouldn't want me, Kathryn, and you certainly shouldn't want me near any child. What would I teach it? To be like me?"

"Stop," she commanded him.

"I'll support you in any way you want me to," he said gruffly. "But I won't be surprised if you think that's a terrible idea."

Kathryn stared at him for a long moment, then made a low, hard sort of noise. She surged forward, wrapping her arms around him. And he couldn't seem to keep himself from folding his own over her, to keep her there.

"My mother lives her whole life in the past, Luca," she whispered fiercely. "Nothing is ever good enough for her, certainly not me." She reached over and took his hand then dragged it to her still-flat belly. "But this baby won't live like that. This baby will be loved. It already is."

He shook his head. "You're both better off without me."

"Luca," she whispered, her voice just as ferocious, "I love you. That isn't going to go away, no matter what you do."

"I don't know what that is," he threw at her. "You should pay attention. I'm a terrible man, Kathryn. Terrible enough to let you take me back, because I want you too much. Terrible enough to keep you when I know I should let you go. What would you call that if not crazy?"

"Love, you idiot," she told him, tears falling down her cheeks again. "I'd call it love."

Luca reached over then and cupped her face between his hands, drawing her closer. Drawing her in, where he'd never thought he'd have her again. Where he would do his best to earn her.

"I think," he said, right there against that mouth of hers, "that you're going to have to show me what you mean. And it might take a while."

And he could feel her smile, right there against his own, and it was like coming home.

"I have a lifetime," she told him.

Which, Luca decided as she pressed her mouth to his at last, was a very good start.

The second time she married a Castelli, it was a bright June day with an achingly beautiful English summer sky arched blue and impossible above them that no one had to tell Kathryn was its own miracle.

She was beginning to depend on miracles.

Kathryn hid her pregnancy, early in its second trimester, behind the grand white dress she hadn't worn to her first wedding. The bells rang out, and the hordes that Luca had insisted upon inviting packed the village church and spilled out into the lane. It was a far cry from the quick trip to the registry office that had comprised her first set of wedding vows.

The paparazzi had hounded them after those pictures, after Luca had come to Yorkshire and they'd worked things out between them. That hounding had taken on the edge of hysteria when Luca had only shrugged one day at the usual set of shouted questions and announced that he and Kathryn Castelli, yes, the widow of his father formerly known as Saint Kate, were engaged.

They'd been back in Rome by then, tucked away in the penthouse he'd insisted she live in with him, and she'd taken it upon herself to warm up a little bit. She'd started with flowers. Lots and lots of flowers. Acrobatic and colorful, splashing warmth and cheer throughout the stark, steel and crisp-lined space.

"How many flowers are too many?" he'd asked the other day, turning in a circle in the center of the massive space.

"They're a metaphor," she'd replied tartly, typing on her tablet. "The more color in this flat, the more love in your cold, cold heart."

"Then, you'd better call the florist and have more delivered," he'd told her, that simmering look in his dark eyes that still made her own heart flip in her chest. "I feel almost empty."

Then he'd showed her how much of a lie that was, right there on the sleek sofa.

"You haven't asked me to marry you, I note," she'd pointed out after the engagement announcement had spilled all over the papers.

"I'm getting around to it," Luca had said, watching her arrange another dramatic bouquet. He'd been cooking dinner, something Kathryn would have said was entirely beneath him.

"Just as you were getting around to telling me you were a gourmet cook?" she'd asked.

"I am a man of intense mystery and many facets,

cucciola mia," he'd told her. "And I cannot eat in restaurants every night of my life."

"This has nothing to do with you and your control issues, I'm sure," she'd replied, and then laughed so hard it had made her ache when he'd thrown a handful of chopped nuts at her.

The paparazzi had carried on chasing them around Rome, until the day Luca had actually paused while out on one of his runs and had answered one of their salacious, impertinent questions.

"How can you live with yourself now that you've seduced your father's wife?" the man had shouted at him.

Luca had smiled. That glorious smile.

"Have you seen her?" he'd asked. "I live with myself just fine."

Kathryn had only rolled her eyes at that one. She'd been far more concerned that she be able to continue working, and to do the things she wanted to do in the company. And she hadn't been above winning that argument by using the heavy artillery.

When she'd finished with Luca, he'd laughed and told her he'd give her anything if she knelt before him just like that and did all of it over again, her mouth and her hands, every day.

"All I want is my own marketing campaign," she'd told him. "This is merely a side benefit."

"Keep this up," he'd replied lazily, "and I'll give you the whole damned company."

She won the respect of most of her coworkers eventually. And the ones who couldn't handle her presence in the office stopped mattering to her and usually stopped working there, too. The day Luca smiled at her across the conference room table after a presentation she'd slaved over and called her brilliant was all that mattered.

Because she'd been right. This was what she'd been meant to do.

Luca had been the one to book the church and take care of all the wedding details.

"You could participate, *cucciola mia*," he'd said once, on a trip to Australia to tour the Barossa Valley. "It's your wedding, too, I hesitate to remind you."

"Wedding?" she'd asked mildly. "What wedding? No one has proposed to me. How could there be a wedding?"

He'd only grinned.

Rose, of course, had been her usual vicious self. But on one of her visits to the little cottage in Yorkshire, Kathryn had abruptly cut her off when she'd started to spew her usual venom.

"You sacrificed for me, Mum," she'd said, holding her mother's gaze so there could be no mistake. "I can never thank you enough for that. That's what mothers do. And I did my best to do my part, too." She'd waved her hands at the cottage where they'd stood. "You'll never want for anything again. I'll always take care of you."

"Aren't you high and mighty now that you've lain with not one but two—"

"Careful," Luca had warned from his position in the far doorway, where he liked to stand while she visited her mother—like her very own emotional bodyguard. "Very, very careful, please."

And Kathryn had understood that it was Luca who had given her the strength to do this at last. To understand that she didn't have to suffer through her mother's rages and nastiness. That she didn't have to participate in this dysfunction. Luca loved her. He wanted to marry her. They were having a baby, and most of the time they were happy together.

She had nothing to prove to anyone, least of all to this angry, bitter woman who should have loved her most.

"If you can't learn to keep a civil tongue in your head, you'll never see your grandchild," Kathryn had told her. "I might choose to subject myself to this out of obligation and devotion, but I'll never let you tear into my baby the way you do me." Rose had sputtered about threats. "That's a promise, Mum. Not a threat. The choice is yours."

And then later, Luca had held her tight and hadn't judged her at all for crying over the childhood she'd never had with Rose.

Kathryn thought she could do no less for him.

She'd gone out of her way to make sure that they spent as much time with Raphael and Lily as possible, because they were the future of the Castelli family, not the grim past that Luca had already survived. She'd come to understand that no matter how lovely Gianni had been to her, he'd been a neglectful father to Luca. But Luca and Rafael were brothers, and they owned the company together, and they loved each other. That was what mattered now.

They'd gone up shortly after Lily had given birth to little baby Bruno, another dark-eyed, dark-haired Castelli male, and stayed at the old manor house for a few days to marinate in the new shape of their family.

"I hate it here," Luca had told her when she'd woken one night to find him standing by the window instead of in bed. "I've always hated it here."

He'd told her of his lonely childhood, of all the ways he'd tried to get his family's attention. Of all those sad years where he'd been left to his own devices, or the tender mercies of the staff, or the frustrations of his stepmothers.

"You're not a child any longer," she'd told him, rolling out of the bed to go to him. She'd sneaked her arms around him and pressed her cheek to his back. "This house is what you make it. It's only a house."

"It always seemed like a curse."

"You can break the curse," she'd promised him. "All you have to do is love me."

"That, *cucciola mia*, is no trouble at all."

And they'd broken more than a few curses that night, driving each other blissfully mad in that great big bed.

In the morning they'd gathered in the library with Rafael and Lily and the small boys, all of them bursting with pride over the new addition. This was the new version of the Castellis, Kathryn had thought. Not the stiff, formal way things had been the first time she'd come here with Gianni. No furious, horrible Luca. None of that pounding confusion because she'd been with the wrong man.

Nothing but love. So much love, in so many forms.

"Are you truly marrying in June?" Lily had asked as they'd sat together on one of the sofas, watching Rafael hold his brand-new son, that Castelli smile of his lighting up the whole of Northern Italy. "That's only a month away."

"Luca is planning a huge wedding to someone," Kathryn had replied with a laugh. "But he has yet to ask anyone in particular, as far as I know. It's very mysterious."

"About that," Luca had said.

She'd looked up to find him standing before her, the whole world in his dark eyes. Then he'd dropped to his knees, and she'd clapped her hands over her mouth. Kathryn had heard Lily's gasp from the sofa beside her, and had sensed more than seen the way Raphael had turned that smile of his their way.

"I love you," Luca had said. "I want to give you the world. I want this baby and I want you, Kathryn, *cucciola mia*, to be my wife and the mother of my children and the best thing in my life, forever. Will you marry me?"

"I don't know," she'd said, looping her arms around his neck and smiling at him with everything she was. "I've grown so fond of you calling me Stepmother. How can I give that up?"

"You won't regret it," he'd promised her, his hard mouth curving and so much light in his dark eyes. "I have far better names for you."

"I love you," she'd whispered. "I think I always have."

"You are the love of my life," he'd said as he'd tugged her hand down from his neck and slipped a ring onto her finger, where it sparkled so brightly it made her feel dazzled. Or perhaps that was him. "You are the reason I know that such things exist. You are my heart, Kathryn."

"Yes," she'd whispered, tears flowing freely down her cheeks. "Always yes, Luca. Always."

And she married him with his brother at his side and her new sister-in-law at hers, because family was what mattered. Their family. The one they'd made, taking what they needed from what they'd been given and leaving the rest behind, where it belonged.

"This life is too beautiful," she told Luca that night,

their first night together as husband and wife. "How can it ever get better than this?"

Four months later, they found out together, when Kathryn gave birth to a marvelous little creature the Castelli family hadn't seen in generations.

A little girl.

"Hold on tight, *cucciola mia*," Luca told her as they sat together on their first night as their own little nuclear family at last.

He held their perfect daughter in his arms, his dark eyes filled with love and light and the whole of their future, right there within reach.

Theirs for the taking, Kathryn thought happily. Theirs, always.

Luca's smile then was big enough to light up the night. "It's only going to get better from here."

And it did.

* * * * *

MILLS & BOON®
Hardback – February 2016

ROMANCE

Leonetti's Housekeeper Bride	Lynne Graham
The Surprise De Angelis Baby	Cathy Williams
Castelli's Virgin Widow	Caitlin Crews
The Consequence He Must Claim	Dani Collins
Helios Crowns His Mistress	Michelle Smart
Illicit Night with the Greek	Susanna Carr
The Sheikh's Pregnant Prisoner	Tara Pammi
A Deal Sealed by Passion	Louise Fuller
Saved by the CEO	Barbara Wallace
Pregnant with a Royal Baby!	Susan Meier
A Deal to Mend Their Marriage	Michelle Douglas
Swept into the Rich Man's World	Katrina Cudmore
His Shock Valentine's Proposal	Amy Ruttan
Craving Her Ex-Army Doc	Amy Ruttan
The Man She Could Never Forget	Meredith Webber
The Nurse Who Stole His Heart	Alison Roberts
Her Holiday Miracle	Joanna Neil
Discovering Dr Riley	Annie Claydon
His Forever Family	Sarah M. Anderson
How to Sleep with the Boss	Janice Maynard

MILLS & BOON®
Large Print – February 2016

ROMANCE

Claimed for Makarov's Baby	Sharon Kendrick
An Heir Fit for a King	Abby Green
The Wedding Night Debt	Cathy Williams
Seducing His Enemy's Daughter	Annie West
Reunited for the Billionaire's Legacy	Jennifer Hayward
Hidden in the Sheikh's Harem	Michelle Conder
Resisting the Sicilian Playboy	Amanda Cinelli
Soldier, Hero...Husband?	Cara Colter
Falling for Mr December	Kate Hardy
The Baby Who Saved Christmas	Alison Roberts
A Proposal Worth Millions	Sophie Pembroke

HISTORICAL

Christian Seaton: Duke of Danger	Carole Mortimer
The Soldier's Rebel Lover	Marguerite Kaye
Return of Scandal's Son	Janice Preston
The Forgotten Daughter	Lauri Robinson
No Conventional Miss	Eleanor Webster

MEDICAL

Hot Doc from Her Past	Tina Beckett
Surgeons, Rivals...Lovers	Amalie Berlin
Best Friend to Perfect Bride	Jennifer Taylor
Resisting Her Rebel Doc	Joanna Neil
A Baby to Bind Them	Susanne Hampton
Doctor...to Duchess?	Annie O'Neil

MILLS & BOON®
Hardback – March 2016

ROMANCE

The Italian's Ruthless Seduction	Miranda Lee
Awakened by Her Desert Captor	Abby Green
A Forbidden Temptation	Anne Mather
A Vow to Secure His Legacy	Annie West
Carrying the King's Pride	Jennifer Hayward
Bound to the Tuscan Billionaire	Susan Stephens
Required to Wear the Tycoon's Ring	Maggie Cox
The Secret That Shocked De Santis	Natalie Anderson
The Greek's Ready-Made Wife	Jennifer Faye
Crown Prince's Chosen Bride	Kandy Shepherd
Billionaire, Boss...Bridegroom?	Kate Hardy
Married for their Miracle Baby	Soraya Lane
The Socialite's Secret	Carol Marinelli
London's Most Eligible Doctor	Annie O'Neil
Saving Maddie's Baby	Marion Lennox
A Sheikh to Capture Her Heart	Meredith Webber
Breaking All Their Rules	Sue MacKay
One Life-Changing Night	Louisa Heaton
The CEO's Unexpected Child	Andrea Laurence
Snowbound with the Boss	Maureen Child

MILLS & BOON®
Large Print – March 2016

ROMANCE

A Christmas Vow of Seduction	Maisey Yates
Brazilian's Nine Months' Notice	Susan Stephens
The Sheikh's Christmas Conquest	Sharon Kendrick
Shackled to the Sheikh	Trish Morey
Unwrapping the Castelli Secret	Caitlin Crews
A Marriage Fit for a Sinner	Maya Blake
Larenzo's Christmas Baby	Kate Hewitt
His Lost-and-Found Bride	Scarlet Wilson
Housekeeper Under the Mistletoe	Cara Colter
Gift-Wrapped in Her Wedding Dress	Kandy Shepherd
The Prince's Christmas Vow	Jennifer Faye

HISTORICAL

His Housekeeper's Christmas Wish	Louise Allen
Temptation of a Governess	Sarah Mallory
The Demure Miss Manning	Amanda McCabe
Enticing Benedict Cole	Eliza Redgold
In the King's Service	Margaret Moore

MEDICAL

Falling at the Surgeon's Feet	Lucy Ryder
One Night in New York	Amy Ruttan
Daredevil, Doctor...Husband?	Alison Roberts
The Doctor She'd Never Forget	Annie Claydon
Reunited...in Paris!	Sue MacKay
French Fling to Forever	Karin Baine

MILLS & BOON®

Why shop at millsandboon.co.uk?

Each year, thousands of romance readers find their perfect read at millsandboon.co.uk. That's because we're passionate about bringing you the very best romantic fiction. Here are some of the advantages of shopping at www.millsandboon.co.uk:

* **Get new books first**—you'll be able to buy your favourite books one month before they hit the shops

* **Get exclusive discounts**—you'll also be able to buy our specially created monthly collections, with up to 50% off the RRP

* **Find your favourite authors**—latest news, interviews and new releases for all your favourite authors and series on our website, plus ideas for what to try next

* **Join in**—once you've bought your favourite books, don't forget to register with us to rate, review and join in the discussions

Visit **www.millsandboon.co.uk**
for all this and more today!